She'd told him it was over, why couldn't he understand that and leave her alone?

A blast from the outdoor buzzer brought her sharply awake. For a moment, her eyes focused on a beige lampshade on the end table as she tried to identify the noise.

Another blast from the buzzer sent chills down her spine. She knew what it was. Who it was. She turned her head to the wall and frowned. He could buzz his head off for all she cared. She'd be damned if she'd answer. Jacob couldn't get into the foyer without her releasing the latch, yet an unexplained fear clutched her stomach, and she drew her knees to her chest. With a yank, she pulled the quilt up over her head.

He had to know she was home. Her car was parked out in front. She wrapped her arms around her middle then dug her fingers into the hollow of her waist. The buzzer sounded again. Her hands flew up and pressed hard against her ears.

She stayed that way until she was sure he had gone. Slowly, she relaxed her legs and brought her head up for air. By now he was probably down at the corner, trying to call from the booth. Too bad. She'd unplugged her phone.

They've been through countless lifetimes together, but they never seem to get it right…

Jesseree Lipton, high-class model, is troubled by weird dreams and visions of past times and strange places she has never been. Blaming it on the stress of her high-pressure job and fast-paced life in 1980s San Francisco, she decides to get away for a while. Breaking up with her drug-addicted boyfriend and taking a leave of absence from her job, Jess leaves everything behind and heads for a Buddhist retreat in the Sierra Nevada Mountains. There she locks horns with Devon Pearson, an East Indian-American instructor. As Jess and Devon struggle to understand both their animosity to each other and their strong physical attraction, they discover that they have been together through many past lives, where they failed to overcome the obstacles set before them. Can these star-crossed lovers cast aside their endless and ageless misunderstandings to achieve enlightenment and everlasting love, or will they be forced to blunder through even more lifetimes together before they finally gain what they seek?

A love story that transcends time.

KUDOS for *Love Everlasting*

In *Love Everlasting* by Norma Lehr, Jesseree Lipton is a high-fashion model with a druggie for a boyfriend. When she starts having strange dreams, even when she's awake, she decides that the stress of her high-pressure life is making her crazy. Breaking up with her boyfriend, who seems to be turning psychotic, she heads for the Sierra Nevada Mountains and a retreat run by Buddhists. There she meets Devon Pearson, who seems determined to hate her. And she doesn't understand why. As she struggles with both her animosity and her attraction for Devon, she learns that she and Devon have been together in many past lives. But they always screw it up so they can never stay together, and this time it doesn't seem to be working out any better. The book has a strong plot with a number of surprises I didn't see coming. It's well written with some thought-provoking concepts and a sweet romance that will warm your heart. ~ *Taylor Jones, Reviewer*

Love Everlasting by Norma Lehr is the story of two people whose love for each other transcends time. Jesseree Lipton and Devon Pearson are star-crossed lovers who have spent lifetimes together, but can never seem to find the happiness they seek. Something or someone always tears them apart. Now they are reunited in this lifetime in San Francisco in 1980, but the prospects are not good for them finally getting it right. They don't even like each other, for one thing, though the physical attraction is strong. And secondly, Jess is having visions and dreams that she doesn't understand. When a friend suggests that she get away for a while, Jess embraces the idea whole-heartedly. She takes a sabbatical from her fashion-modeling job, breaks up with her drug-addicted lawyer boyfriend, and heads for a Buddhist commune in the California mountains where Devon teaches spiritualism. He doesn't want her there, but he's not in charge and she's allowed to stay. They clash often, but as Jess unwinds and begins her journey of self-discovery, she learns that she and Devon have been down this road before, and it ends badly every time. *Love Everlasting* is a poignant and intriguing story of loss, love, and the lessons we need to learn as humans. The characters are charming, the plot's interesting, and it has enough twists and turns to keep you hooked from the beginning. *~ Regan Murphy, Reviewer*

ACKNOWLEDGEMENTS

Many thanks to my special editors, Faith and Lauri—and also to Jack for the great Tree of Life book cover.

Love
Everlasting

NORMA LEHR

A Black Opal Books Publication

GENRE: PARANORMAL ROMANCE/ROMANTIC SUSPENSE

This is a work of fiction. Names, places, characters and incidents are either the product of the author's imagination or are used fictitiously, and any resemblance to any actual persons, living or dead, businesses, organizations, events or locales is entirely coincidental. All trademarks, service marks, registered trademarks, and registered service marks are the property of their respective owners and are used herein for identification purposes only. The publisher does not have any control over or assume any responsibility for author or third-party websites or their contents.

DEDICATION

To Ramona, my daughter and spiritual traveler

Vivian and Madlynne—my spiritual teachers

Prologue

The Lost Continent:

Caho-Fan bent low over her devoted scribe stretched out on the wide wooden pallet. His head rested on his arms and he groaned with pleasure as she tenderly massaged his feet with scented oil from a round clay vessel.

The sultry air hanging heavy in the Great Temple of Knowledge lent itself to the desires of the flesh as Caho-Fan's fingers, heavily ringed with jewels, kneaded the oily pool into his ankles. She worked his solid calves, rose to his thighs, then upward to his broad back, caressing his muscles beneath his firm skin.

In the distance through the arches of her private

chambers, dark billows of smoke from volcanic eruptions rose tall against the sky. Closer in, sea water filled with charred debris lapped against the mammoth steps of the stone temple, and she shuddered, recalling the last deluge as it rushed toward the columned entrance to the east. Once again her mind's eye beheld the terrible shaking cataclysm. Buildings and earth crumbled in one gigantic rumble, heaving, and submerging great chunks of land and its screaming masses to their fate beneath the sea.

Now the dark waters rose again. Those who had survived the sinking continent had gone ahead. They had left in haste to reach higher ground, seeking safety on the plateaus.

A low groan from the scribe brought her back to the present, and she began rubbing vigorously with longer strokes. Her breath came in small gasps.

Turning on his side, he reached up and held her wrists. "I must leave now, Caho-Fan. It is late." His dark eyes filled with despair. "The last ship to Egyo awaits me at the dock."

She trembled as he pressed her fingers to his lips. "No. No," she pleaded." Do not leave me, my love, my life. A cruel future awaits me without you to guide me."

Lowering herself next to him on the pallet, she pulled him close to her carefully scented body and brushed his mouth with her lips. "Come with me to the High Mountain," she whispered. "Together we will build the new temple. A new empire."

"But my destiny lies with the colony." He slowly shook his head. "I must follow the papyrus scrolls to the temple in the east. I am the only one left to transcribe the symbols. My work is there on the far side of the world."

Caho-Fan wept silently. Her warm tears fell on his bare shoulder. He held her close while he tried to console her.

"At a future time we will be together again," he promised. "But for now your destiny is to rule. Mine is to go." He wiped her tears with his fingers. "Do not forget you are a daughter of a God, while I am only a son of man. The betrothal to your half-brother has been record-ed."

"Then the edict must be altered, "she cried. "I will bow before the Council and beg that you be sent away with me."

"Ah, my priestess. With all your power and wisdom, you are ignorant to the ways of men. It matters not what the Council decrees. You forget that your half-brother is a man." The scribe's eyes narrowed. "And a cunning one. Even with his youth, he senses our bond. He would fol-low and destroy us if we choose that path." He leaned back. "My Goddess, daughter of the Rain God, Tec-Tal, no man is worthy of you. When your mother requested to conceive of the Gods, she vowed her offspring would rule the High Lands when the prophecy of the great flood came upon us. The Gods and your mother are aware that the time is near. It is recorded that we all leave swiftly."

"Then I order you to come with me," she cried, pulling him to her. "I will hide you beneath the linens in the ten wheeled cart. When my brother discovers you have journeyed with us, he will be helpless." She lifted her chin in a regal pose. "I will have all the power. No one will listen to his childish cries of anger. The Tribunal will have sailed for the colony and the Council chooses to sink into the sea with the Crystal."

"And what of your mother? She has power as the High Priestess."

"My mother." Caho-Fan turned away and wept softly. "Mother wishes to leave her ageing body to the ravages of the final cataclysm. Oh, beloved. Do you not see? I cannot go forth to lead new tribes without your strength and wisdom. My mother will be gone. My brother is too young. He holds no vision. I need you."

He stared up at the gossamer purple fabric draped across the stone ceiling. She closed her eyes, summoning the power bequeathed her by her father, Tec-TAl. She rose from the pallet and stood stately. An effusion of light beamed from her spiritual eye. Loosening the gold bejeweled girdle encircling her waist, she shook free of her white robe, allowing it to cascade around her feet. With her chin held high, she stepped forth leaving the garment behind on the marble floor. Lifting her slender fingers to the nape of her neck, she removed two shell combs releasing a thick halo of hair to fall around her shoulders and breasts like a golden sheath.

In the dim smoky light of mid-day, she lowered her naked body beside him on the pallet. Drawing him into her circle of shimmering light, she held him as the earth trembled beneath the temple floors.

Chapter 1

San Francisco, 1980:

Click: "Jess, stand still."

Click—click: "Fix her lipstick, it's smeared again."

Click: "Chin down—look up. Up here—damn, Jess, look alive. Closer to the fans—hair's not blowing. I want a sea breeze!"

"Jess. Jess!"

The platform shifted. A wavelike motion caught her, pushed her off balance. No more platforms. Only sinking sand.

"Grab her, for Chrissake. Will someone grab her hands?"

She groped, reached up, and screamed. And screamed and screamed.

෴

Jesseree bolted up in bed. Her heart pounded in her throat. Spastic breaths held her spine erect as she pressed her forehead with a clammy palm, pasting strands of blond hair to her face. Her fingers clutched her throat in an attempt to still the throbbing. Squinting through the darkness she searched for something familiar.

Where were the cameras? The photographers?

She jumped as a gust of wind flapped a curtain at the open window above her. A strong salty smell from the bay blew in, rustling the sheet next to her thigh. Aware now that she lay next to Jacob, she sank back on the damp pillow with relief while she struggled to calm her breath.

Don't wake him, she told herself. *Let him sleep.*

This dream, the same one for months now, scared her. Each time the terror of sinking grew worse. What did it mean? She was losing sleep and it showed. Lately when she looked in the mirror, she could count the light crow's feet forming around her eyes. Could be this sinking dream meant she felt panic about her age. Twenty-eight wasn't old, but in her business, models were forced to look young forever in front of the camera or lose their jobs.

Valium. That's what she needed. A call to her therapist in the morning would get her a refill. But what about tomorrow? She had a shoot in the morning. How would she manage to work with no sleep? And this client? One of the worst. Their booze ads demanded the models look bright and sexy to sell their product.

She allowed herself another few minutes of rest before sliding her long legs over the side of the bed. In two strides, she reached the bathroom.

"Hey. What's going on?" Jacob Kelso rose up on his elbow, blinking at the light.

"Gotta go home," she called through the cracked door.

He flopped back down. "Why?"

"I've got a shoot in the morning. If I go to sleep here, I'll never make it."

"Set the alarm," he snapped. "You can get up." He turned his face to the wall.

What was his problem now? She didn't have time for this. For the last month he'd been intolerable. Nothing she did pleased him. She shook her head and sighed. He certainly wasn't the same person she'd started dating six months ago.

"Sorry, Kelso," she called out. "I'll see you tonight. The party for Lee. Remember?"

She opened the bathroom door and, after a quick run of her fingers through hair, zipped up her jeans, and grabbed her oversize leather bag from a chair.

"Be sure and wear your boogie shoes," she added. "The party's at Oz."

She waited a moment. When he didn't reply, she shrugged and left.

The San Francisco fog veiled and distorted the familiar landmarks that guided Jesseree the two blocks from Jacob's place to hers. Buildings, pole lights, and storefronts suddenly loomed out of nowhere as she made her way along Lombard Street. This neighborhood, close to the Marina, was considered safe. But still, on a foggy night, everything appeared eerie.

Still haunted by her dream, she switched her thoughts to Jacob. Why did she put up with him and his problems when she had enough of her own? His mood swings and his possessiveness were driving her crazy. Last month, she'd been to see Paula, her therapist, twice a week instead of the usual once.

Jacob might be a brilliant law student, but he could act the fool when it came to her. She should be able to tell him about this recurring nightmare without his nasty verbal pokes. One night at his place, when she awoke in a sweat, she had tried, really tried to make him understand how real the dream was, and how terrified it made her feel when she started to sink, but he had only grinned and spit out that it must be time for her to see her therapist again, at old "Paula's pad for psychos."

With a sarcastic snort, he'd begin his lecture again about how he could settle all of her problems if they got married. "When I've finished my studies, you won't have to work. It's your job that makes you crazy."

He could be right about her job, but not about marriage. She wasn't anywhere close to that kind of commitment. And the more time she spent alone with Jacob, the firmer her resolve became that marriage to him would never happen.

As she entered the foyer of the green stucco apartment building she called home, she sighed with relief. Her refuge. She dug her keys from her bag and unlocked the first door on her left. Once inside, she collapsed into the recliner. Glancing at her watch, she moaned. In five short hours she'd be back on the merry-go-round again.

Her stomach growled, but she forced her eyes away from the kitchen, confirming with a nod that tomorrow every ounce would photograph like a pound. The hunger pangs clamped hard in her middle, and she pulled her knees to her chest. Placing her head on the arm of the plush chair, she closed her eyes and fell asleep.

ೞೞ

The outside elevator of the St. Francis Hotel jetted toward the top floor, sending city lights tumbling like diamonds spilled from a giant bucket. The designer couples sardined in the swift moving glass box, chatted with excitement.

Jesseree gazed out at the nighttime splendor dramatically spread at her feet. San Francisco after dark. Breath-taking. She stood next to Jacob at the back of the elevator and looked down at his face. Conscious of her height when he escorted her, she usually wore dressy flats, but tonight she wore two inch heels. He had already complained. Let him! Her sensational outfit called for height. A number of top models and their agents would be attending this party tonight, and she was expected by her modeling agency to look striking.

She adjusted her cinnamon satin sash, feeling comfortably chic in Giorgio Armani's black Japanese pajama. Delighted with her choice, she planned to be a standout. She nodded to herself. Stunning! That's what this big time fashion game was all about.

Jacob pressed close to her, his eyes already murky from drink. "Don't wander off without me, Jess, okay?"

Good Lord, she thought. He's already making demands. Well, he better cool his drinking. If he did anything tonight to embarrass her, she swore she'd leave him for good.

"Your hair, Jacob." She attempted to change the subject. "Who styled it?"

"A little place on Union." His eyes narrowed." Why? What's wrong with it?"

"Nothing." She raised her shoulders. "You really have great hair. That's all. It takes lots of bucks to have mine done right."

The elevator jarred to a stop and the doors hummed

open. The small talk ended and she vowed to be patient as she followed the flow of glitter into the fabulous Disco called OZ.

Chapter 2

Before Jesseree could turn around, Jacob had darted off, elbowing his way through the crowd to the bar.

She knew he was nervous because the guest of honor was a man he admired, but then lately it seemed that any social occasion they attended called for him to have multiple drinks in advance to sustain him. She just hoped and prayed that he would cool it tonight.

This celebration for Lee Cramer, a VIP defense attorney, was held in honor of his fiftieth birthday, and the disco was packed with San Francisco's elite. His gorgeous wife, Cindy Brockhurst, known only to the media as Cindy, worked out of Kurlay Agency, the same as Jesseree, and an open invitation to attend this party had been posted at the reception desk for all Kurlay models and their escorts.

Jacob's first reaction to the invitation had been one of elation to be on scene where he might make career contacts with everyone who was anyone. But later his mood plummeted to self-pity, whining to Jesseree that no one would be interested in a third year law student. And now that they had finally arrived, he had left the elevator and sauntered off without her. Strange, after his plea coming up in the elevator for her not to leave him.

She wandered over near the bar while she waited for him to join her. Standing there alone, she caught bits of laughter and friendly conversation from the milling crowd as the party guests in their designer clothes pushed past her. She stepped back and caught her breath as she scanned the decor of the room. This Disco Oz, with its white oversized sofas, glass tables, shimmering windows and mirrors, had a feeling of a winter wonderland with endless space. She gazed past the crowd to the windows and into the night. Suddenly a hollow feeling in her stomach made her wonder what her life was all about, and she strongly wished with all of her heart that this second she was somewhere else, not here. Where? She hadn't a clue. Just somewhere.

A plate of hors d'oeuvres passed by and she helped herself to one round shaped crust-less sandwich and two tiny triangles. She decided to eat tonight, try to get rid of that hollow feeling and worry about it tomorrow. Five years ago when she'd began modeling she didn't have to be concerned about her weight. But now—must be her age. Already tired of counting daily calories, she wondered what it would be like in a few years from now when she turned thirty. She shivered at the thought.

Couples flocked to the dance floor. The women's colorful clothes brought a bazaar-like atmosphere to the room's frozen decor. She watched as metallic colors flashed across the walls and ceiling, while pulsating lights caused the dancers' movements to appear forced and jerky.

She felt a tap on her arm and turned to the smiling face of her friend, Maureen. "Jess, you look fantastic. What a super outfit."

"Maureen. I'm so glad you're here." She glanced over Maureen's shoulder. "Did you bring your new friend?

"You bet. Phillip's got a table for us. Come on. I want him to meet you."

As they eased their way over to the other side of the room, Jesseree made a quick search for Jacob. Nowhere in sight. She attempted to shake off her concern as she realized Maureen, the receptionist at Kurlay, was just the lively person she needed to be with right now. Five days a week all business, the person all the models counted on, handling the agency on a daily basis in an organized manner. But on weekends? Another Maureen emerged as she embraced her counter-culture consciousness. A real freeze-dried hippy, she labeled herself, who lived in a small cottage with a flourishing organic vegetable garden in Marin. Jesseree had been invited over for lunch and spent last weekend there. After arriving on Saturday, kicking off her shoes and following Maureen outside to a brick patio, some of the stress in Jesseree's life had vanished. Even thoughts of her waning relationship with Jacob had eased as she grabbed a spade and worked alongside Maureen, planting bulbs and pulling weeds.

Maureen's philosophy? Give it all you've got for five, and then do what you love for two. Jesseree sighed. She wanted that. But in her line of work, except for an occasional weekend away from the modeling game, her time was always scheduled.

As they approached the table, Phillip stood. He slid an arm around Maureen's waist and nodded to Jesseree.

Maureen's eye sparkled with pride. "You've got to know who this is, Phillip."

"I most certainly know your work, Jesseree. It's my pleasure to meet you in person."

Phillip, a new fashion photographer in the city, was quickly gaining a name for himself in the business, and Maureen seemed to genuinely adore him.

Phillip glanced behind her as they sat down. "Are you here alone?"

"No way." Maureen's eyes widened. "She's almost engaged to Jacob Kelso." She looked around uncertainly. "Where is that guy?"

Jesseree shuddered at the word engaged. Where did Maureen get that idea? "He's around here somewhere."

Maureen searched the room. "He's probably looking for you."

Jesseree nodded. "I'll wander over to the bar. That's where he headed."

As she slid from the sofa, Jacob suddenly appeared out of the crowd and headed toward the table with two drinks, one in each hand. He grinned and waved, unmindful of the full glass. She cringed as huge spurts of booze splashed on the pale carpet.

"Hi, everyone. Where did you disappear to, Jess? I've been searching all over for you." He stumbled forward and put his arm around her waist. The glass tipped and ice slid down the back of her designer top.

He grinned. "Whoops."

Jesseree glared at him, turned, and fled. Maureen followed, both heading for the women's lounge, leaving Jacob with Phillip.

Once inside, Maureen blotted the spill with paper towels. "He didn't mean it, Jess. He's a little bombed."

Jesseree grabbed a towel and helped. "He's been drinking since before we left my place."

"So? What's the big deal? Your top isn't ruined." She stuffed the damp towels in the chrome trash bin. "He's just having a good time."

Jesseree snorted. "Well, I'm not."

Maureen glanced up. "Why?"

Jesseree shook her head. "He makes me upset. Sick, really."

Maureen studied Jesseree's reflection in the mirror. "You're really mad, huh?"

Jesseree gave a sharp nod.

Maureen motioned to the door. "Come on. Let's get him out on the dance floor. A little movement will clear his head."

Jesseree cradled her elbows. "You go on ahead. I'll be out in a few minutes."

Maureen hesitated at the door. It swung open and two laughing women in high maintenance gowns, one gold lame the other jade green, entered the lounge, accompanied by a blast of disco. As they squeezed past, Maureen slid by them and waved with concern at Jesseree. The door closed and the women hurried to the mirrors with globe lights and proceeded to chat as they repaired their makeup.

Jesseree moved over to a chaise lounge, slipped off her heels and elevated her feet. Five minutes of rest might help. She closed her eyes and draped a hand across her brow.

Shakespeare's lines flooded her mind. *All the world is a stage and all the men and women in it are merely players*

Maybe that was it. Her life—a bizarre production. All of this mess tonight with Jacob, just another scene that she had played out before. Looking back, some of the times she'd spent with him seemed like repeats. Some of their conversations came across to her as old script from another time and place.

When she had mentioned this to her therapist, Paula said it could be collective consciousness. Inheriting memories from her ancestors. Jesseree had found that a confusing concept and, without trying to figure it out, let it drop.

The door swung open again and a young woman shimmied in to the beat of the music, prompting Jesseree to get back to the party. She stood and slid into her strappy gold heels. Removing a small brush from her evening bag, she fluffed up the back of her light hair. Using a lipstick pencil, she carefully outlined her lips. After an approving glance in the gold-rimmed mirror, she placed a hand over her middle and took in a deep breath.

From the doorway, she could see Jacob sitting at the table alone. She slowly approached him and stopped. A murky shade of gray surrounded his head. The wreath extended out nearly a foot and shimmered darkly. Good Lord! She glanced away. When she looked back, the ring hovered like a muddy halo. Jacob had been slouched watching the dancers.

When he spotted her, he began motioning for her to join him. She braced herself and continued on. "Where are Maureen and Phillip?" She tried to sound calm.

Jacob pointed to the dance floor and patted the seat next to him.

Ignoring his pat on the chair, she sat across the table from him.

He frowned. "Why are you way over there?"

"So we can talk." The ring of darkness began to fade. Sipping her drink, she watched him above the rim of her glass.

"Good show, Jess," he spat with contempt. Red and black jagged barbs spiked out from his throat area like flashing neon. "You really enjoy making me look like an ass."

He stared at her over the rim of his glass while he downed his drink.

Jesseree covered her mouth with her hand, took a deep breath, and shook her head in disbelief.

"And what's with this guy Phillip? Is he another one of your admirers?"

Jesseree found her voice "I think he admires my work."

His voice lowered, still thick with suspicion. "You pose for him, don't you?"

She straightened in her seat. "What is wrong with you? I met him here for the first time tonight."

"Don't feed me that crap. You constantly hide things from me. I saw the way he looks at you."

"He's probably studying my clothes." She hated this. Always having to defend herself when she was with him. "This jewelry I'm wearing is an original design." Her fingers clutched at the copper and crystal necklace roped about her neck. "He's a new photographer. That's how he learns."

His eyes narrowed. "I'll bet there are a few more things you'd enjoy teaching him. Right?"

She ignored his obscene remark as the darkness around his head grew in intensity. She jumped up. "Come on, Kelso. Let's not argue." She forced herself to move to his side of the table and lift his clenched hand. "Let's dance."

His grip tightened. She glanced down. "What's in your hand?" She dropped down next to him. "What is it?"

His grip relaxed and she unfolded his fingers. A cocaine vial flashed in his open palm. He shifted his fingers and a tiny metal spoon suddenly released and dangled from a short silver chain. It spun hypnotically like an ancient symbol of doom.

"Where did you get it?" she demanded. "How dare you bring this here?"

"What d'ya mean? I got it here. There's more being passed around."

Close enough now to smell his metallic breath, she backed away.

"Get off it, Jess. Grow up." He pushed the vial close to her face. "Try it."

"Stop it." She moved to the other side of the table and glared at him. "You really are an ass."

He thrust his arm across the table. The vial jiggled in his open hand. She swatted at his arm and the glass tube flew out and hit the carpet. He leaned over, snagged it, unwound the tangled chain, and dusted it off with his fingertips. Glaring in defiance, he placed the tube on the table between them.

"Put it away, Jacob."

"Why? It's no different than those goddamn pills your shrink prescribes. The ones that make you act nuts." He leaned back. "You know what? I'm getting tired of your sanctimonious bullshit."

The Valium. She should have guessed. She started to explain once more about her nightmares then suddenly stopped. This whole scene was insane. A sudden flash of insight told her she didn't have to explain anything to him. She didn't have to talk to Jacob Kelso ever again. This neurotic hanging on to a sinking relationship was over.

She looked at his contorted face and his cocaine-brightened eyes and knew this was the end. The end of her and Jacob and all the lame excuses she'd invented to stick with him. This exit should have been made a long time ago. The murkiness still hung around his head, making it difficult to define where he stopped and it began. Brushing aside an angry sadness, she knew there had to be something better in life than this. Tonight was the last scene of their final performance. This show had been running far too long.

She grabbed her evening bag and stood. "It's over, Jacob."

"Sit down," he demanded. "Stop overreacting."

She glared down at him. "I never want to see you again. Don't phone or come to my place. Don't wait for me at work. Understand?" She turned to leave.

"Wait. What about our wedding? All of our plans?"

"Your plans," she said. "Not mine."

His face turned ashen. "You're not serious."

She gave a firm nod. "Dead serious."

He fell back against the chair. By now groups at surrounding tables sensed trouble and watched them with spaced-out curiosity.

Jesseree ignored them all as she started for the elevator.

He rushed up behind and grabbed her arm, forcing her to face him. "How do you expect me to get home? You're driving."

She wrenched herself away. "Take a cab."

With a shaky finger she reached out and pressed the button. The elevator instantly appeared and she bolted aboard as the doors closed. She turned toward the city lights but this time with an unseeing rage. Her senses, wiped out by fury, now suddenly sharpened by a twisting foot pain. She stumbled over, grabbed the metal rail for support, and looked down. The heel of her shoe had broken off and the soft tissue of her ankle was swelling.

"Good grief." she cried out. "What else?" She felt a lurch and hung on as the box swiftly made its decent.

Chapter 3

The San Francisco night air hit Jesseree like a tidal wave of relief. She sucked in deep breaths of the cool moisture and hobbled out to the street. The pain in her right ankle kept her disoriented while she tried to remember where she'd left her car. She thought about hailing a taxi, but then how would she get back to her car in the morning? Who knew? She might not be able to walk by then. Perspiration dotted her forehead. Union Square. Right! She'd parked there.

She limped along, hugging the sides of the building until she hopped across at the intersection. Inching her way down the parking ramp, she spotted the silver sports car and struggled on until she reached her Nissan.

She dropped into the seat and cradled her throbbing

ankle with the skin pulled taut. Using her fingertips, she explored the protruding mass. The foot needed to be wrapped and she rummaged through the glove box. Nothing. Not even a Band-Aid. She eased up, and a hook from her sash caught on the ridge of the seat. Unwinding the sash from her waist, she carefully used it to wrap her ankle working the stretchy fabric smooth starting above the toes. Now with some support, her foot might be able to handle the gas pedal.

She switched on the ignition and rotated her knee. Using the ball of her foot and toes, she pressed down. The engine roared, echoing through the underground arena as she backed out and headed up the ramp.

She stayed in the slow lane and rolled down her window. The cold night air whipped at her face. Damn Jacob. Accusing her of overreacting. Tonight had been the last straw. She gave a sharp nod. Never in this world would she put up with a user. She'd seen too many people in her business go down the tubes. Now that it had finally ended between them, she wished the agony of tonight would go away. Heading north on Van Ness, she missed her turn at Lombard and wound up following the traffic toward the bay. She punched on the radio. Montovani. Her grandmother's favorite.

She felt lost now, tonight, but she'd really have been lost years ago if it hadn't been for Grandma. When her parents drowned off Coyote Point, she was barely more than a toddler, but she remembered the funeral.

Grownups in the kitchen. Grandma sobbing for her only daughter. Blaming Jesseree's dad and his drinking for the boating accident.

Four years old had been a crucial age to lose one's parents. During weekly sessions with Paula, the therapist had explained to her that her fear of abandonment now probably stemmed from that childhood trauma. At times, Jesseree's years of growing up seemed long ago. Other times like tonight, she felt like a child again, stumbling her way through a sophisticated life-style

Lost in her thoughts, she cruised past another cutoff. The Golden Gate Bridge loomed ahead. No more off ramps. No choice now except to follow the traffic.

Her mind slipped back to her job, which pressed on her mind constantly. She couldn't let down or let go, even on her days off. One false move on her part and Mr. Crandal would fill her place at the agency with one of a dozen other younger models waiting on the sidelines. If she could only let go and rest her mind. What she really needed? A long talk with her grandmother in Arizona, but it was too late to call tonight.

A fog screen settled on the bridge. She turned on the wipers and rolled the window part way up. Her foot cramped, causing her to wince. When she turned her toes too quickly, the pain caused her foot to slip from the pedal. She must be crazy, crossing the bridge on a Saturday night with her foot in a velvet sash sling.

A black Porsche honked her aside, coming dangerously close to swiping her door as it passed. It cut in front of her then vanished into the fog. The profile of the driver reminded her of Jacob. "Go ahead and hit me," she cried. "Jerk!"

At Oz, Jacob had said he was tired of her sanctimonious bullshit. What was that about? Sanctimonious because she refused to use his drug of choice? She shook her head in disbelief. Let him steep in his booze and drugs. After tonight, she was finally free of him.

She eased the car off the bridge on the Marin side, blinked hard and started to cry. Unable to see through the puddles of blurred lights, she pulled over to the side of the road. Leaning her head against the leather steering wheel, she surrendered to the weeping she'd been holding back. When she finally looked up, a road sign on her left pointed two miles to Sausalito. Wiping her eyes and nose with a tissue, she repositioned her foot on the pedal.

Sarah lived in Sausalito. Sarah Brunson, her grandmother's friend. The closest person Jesseree had in her life next to Grandma. She peered at the numbers on the dash clock. Eleven thirty. Too late? She'd drive by Sarah's house and look for a light. Easing the long nosed sports car back into the heavy traffic, she headed down the hill

❧❧❧

"Jesseree. Child. Come in." The door widened and

Sarah's arms encircled her. Warm kisses caressed her face.

Jesseree returned the hugs and kisses then gave an extra squeeze to her old friend. Closing her eyes, she held on tight as the tears surfaced again. "Is it too late for a visit?"

Sarah closed the door behind her. "Never too late for you." She brushed her long graying hair back from her face then held Jesseree at arm's length. "Let me look at you, dear. It's been way too long."

Jesseree buried her head in Sarah's shoulder. A familiar scent clung to the older woman's robe, evoking pleasant memories of childhood.

Sarah patted Jesseree's back. "Come on, dear." She led her into the front room. "Let's get by the fire where it's warm."

Jesseree limped along behind her. A smoldering log in the fireplace and small table lamp gave off a dim light to the room. Her eyes fixed on a large wall painting of the snowy Himalayas. A two-story monastery nestled in the layered pines, dwarfed by the massive background of mountains and sky. She remembered gazing at this painting many times before, but now the picture drew her in.

Sarah leaned over. "What on earth? Is that a bandage on your foot or a new style of sandal?"

Jesseree gazed down at her foot. "I hurt myself."

Sarah supported Jesseree's arm as she helped her over to the sofa. "Let's get that foot elevated." She placed a pillow under the foot then proceeded to unwind the sash. "It's wrapped too tight." She fluffed up another pillow and slipped it behind Jesseree's head. "Relax now while I prepare a compress." She climbed the two steps to the open kitchen then poured water into a cast-iron kettle. "Is rosehip tea still your favorite?"

Jesseree nodded. She didn't care much for herb tea at all, but she drank rosehip when she visited Sarah. A flame leaped up, catching onto a sliver of wood. The room brightened, helping to lift Jesseree's mood.

Sarah brought the tea down and placed it on a small oval table. "The compress will be ready soon." Her fingers tenderly pressed the swollen area on the ankle, causing Jesseree to flinch. When Sarah returned for the compress, her slippers slapped against the wooden steps. She cut a large swath of cheesecloth and placed something from her cupboard in the center. Folding in the sides, she tore off a piece of plastic wrap from a box. When everything got placed on an ebony tray, she came back and sat on the end of the sofa. She slipped the plastic under Jesseree's foot and smoothed the compress over the ankle.

"This is a comfrey root compress. The swelling should be almost gone by morning." Sarah settled back into a comfortable spot on her rocker, "Now. Tell me what happened."

Jesseree explained what went on at Oz. She cried at times then laughed at others.

Sarah listened with interest. When Jesseree got to the part about the wreath around Jacob's head, Sarah lifted a finger. "You saw his aura. Not everyone can see them you know. It's a gift."

Jesseree sniffed as she wiped her nose with a tissue. "Do you see them?"

"Sometimes. They're not always dark. Our auras turn murky when our motives aren't pure."

Jesseree sipped at her tea. "That awful dark color—was that part of Jacob?"

Sarah nodded. "The aura is our energy. It lives and moves. It's an extension of our physical body."

Jesseree scooted up and put the pillow at the small of her back. "Where does it come from?"

"From our Higher Power. Spiritual teachers have known about auras for thousands of years." Sarah reached over and adjusted the compress on Jesseree's foot. "The state of our health, our desires, ideas, moods, feelings, all manifest out in energy colors. It's really to our advantage to make our auras the color of rainbows."

Jesseree had a feeling Sarah studied her aura as they spoke.

Sarah pushed herself up from the rocker and crossed to the fireplace. She lifted a good-sized log from the tub on the hearth and placed the wood on the grate. At seventy, she stands so straight, Jesseree thought. She watched as Sarah stoked the fire then pulled her robe close around her sturdy legs. "Aside from these problems with Jacob, how are you feeling?" She turned to face her. "Are you eating well? Exercising? When you were a youngster, I taught you techniques to meditate. Remember? Do you use those techniques now?"

Before Jesseree had a chance to reply, a movement at the hall entrance caught her eye. A tall man at the shadowy end of the room stood silently observing them. His wide shoulders filled the doorway, his arms relaxed at his sides.

"Devon." Sarah pulled a chair close to the fire. "I thought you were asleep. Come in and join us. Meet my oldest friend's granddaughter."

Jesseree looked over at Sarah with surprise. "I didn't realize you had company."

Sarah grasped her guest's hand. "Jesseree. This is my dear friend, Devon."

Chapter 4

Jesseree looked up into dark, almond-shaped eyes. Sarah's guest stood with his back to the fire and a golden glow radiated around him. He wore cotton drawstring pants and a long sleeved top a shade lighter than his tan skin. He bowed. "It's a pleasure to meet you, Jesseree."

A pleasant sensation stirred within when he spoke her name. But why so formal? He remained standing though Sarah offered the chair. When Sarah explained to him about Jesseree's accident, he moved over to the sofa. In the shifting light from the fire, his smooth bare feet appeared bronze. He adjusted the lotus shade on the lamp and then without touching her leg, examined her foot.

For a fraction of a moment, Jesseree had the crazy

urge to reach out and touch his dark hair, but restrained herself. Who is he and what was he doing here at Sarah's? She hoped she wasn't expected to chat with him tonight, because she most certainly wasn't herself and really didn't feel like visiting with anyone except Sarah.

But chatting with this guy didn't happen because he studiously ignored her as he spoke quietly to Sarah. Jesseree strained to hear what he said, but his low voice didn't rise above the crackling of the fire. Without a word to her, or a look in her direction, he turned and left the room.

"Devon's gone to get something that will help reduce the swelling," Sarah said.

Jesseree shook her head. "Uh-uh. No. I don't think I want him to put anything on my foot."

Sarah put a finger to her lips. "Let him help you. He knows what he's doing. And I'll be right here."

"Who is he?"

"I've known him and his father for years. Trust me, Jesseree. Please."

Devon returned with a small bottle of reddish brown liquid. Jesseree eyes narrowed. "What are you planning to do?"

"Apply this liniment to your ankle," His voice was firm with an edgy tone. "It will relieve your pain." He focused on her ankle while he shook the bottle. Kneeling on the carpet, he slid his warm fingers under her foot. "Now take a deep breath."

She looked over at Sarah. Sarah nodded. Jesseree filled her lungs as he directed then released the air all at once.

"Now. Again."

She did and leaned her head back on the cushion.

Devon handed the bottle to Sarah. She released the cap and poured the liniment into the palm of his cupped hand. He gazed into the oily pool before angling his hand, allowing a stream of copper pearls to trickle across the swelling. He covered her ankle with his large hand then closed his eyes. Jesseree glanced up at Sarah and her eyes were closed too. The room became still. The only sounds? The occasional movements in the fireplace and the slow shallow breathing of Sarah and Devon.

A few minutes passed before he removed his hand. When he did, Sarah opened her eyes and went over to the chair next to the fire.

"Now." Devon reached out. "Give me your hand again."

Sounded more like a command than a request. "What for?" Jesseree avoided his eyes.

"There's a pressure point there that will relieve the pain." She held out her hand. He stood so close to her now that she could smell the incense on his shirt. He placed her thumb and forefinger together making a fleshy mound. "Now Relax it." He firmly probed the area.

She winced.

"This point is sensitive."

She tried to pull away. "Right."

He manipulated the pressure point another few seconds before he released her.

Frowning, she massaged her hand. "That really hurt. It still does."

Sarah came over. "It won't for long," She patted Jesseree's arm. "Try to remember where that pressure point is. You can massage it to relieve all kinds of pain."

Devon put the cap back on the bottle.

Jesseree squinted. "What's in there?

"Herbal tincture." He bowed again and excused himself.

"Thank you," Jesseree mumbled as he left the room. When she was sure he'd gone, she flooded Sarah with questions. "Who is he? Does he live around here? Do I detect a slight accent?"

"Wait." Sarah smiled. "I can't keep up with you. His father was a good friend of mine a long time ago. When I stayed in India, he worked there for the United States."

Jesseree vaguely remembered talk years ago of Sarah's trip. "Is Devon East Indian?"

"Half. His mother is from Varanasi, a Holy City on the Ganges. His father met his mother when he worked there and they were married. When Devon was twelve, his father transferred back to this country." Sarah stirred the fire. "Devon is really a very fascinating blend of East and West."

"Well," Jesseree sniffed. "I appreciate his effort but personally I found him rude."

Sarah stared at the fire. "I know sometimes he seems abrupt. I believe he thinks most American women are pampered and spoiled. He's never said as much but it's something I pick up on."

Snobbish, Jesseree thought. "Does he live in the city?"

"He teaches at a retreat in the Sierra. This last week he's been lecturing in the Bay Area. That's why he's here. When he comes to the city, I insist he stay with me. He's such a love."

Jesseree didn't agree. She wasn't accustomed to such a cool dismissal. But he must be a healer. She glanced down at her foot. It felt better already.

"More tea?" Sarah gathered up the cups.

"No thanks. But do you suppose I could stay the night?"

"I wouldn't think of letting you drive back to the city this time of night." She pulled up an Afghan from the foot of the sofa. "I'm afraid you'll have to sleep with some of your clothes on. There's no way we could get the tight hem of those pants over that ankle."

Jesseree frowned and peered down the hall that led to the guest room. If he wasn't here she could sleep comfortably in that bed. Oh, well!

Sarah sat down. "Let's talk for a while."

Jesseree felt exhausted, but she knew Sarah might

have sage thoughts to share. She eased herself back to a sitting position.

Sarah began slowly as if weighing every word. "I've been thinking over what you've said, dear, and I believe that the answer to your problems is love. Love can change your attitude in working out problems that seem unsolvable. Love also has a funny way of loosening one's emotional knots too."

"I wish I could feel love for Jacob." Jesseree shook her head. "And also for my job, but I can't. That's why I see a therapist." A sudden sadness filled her heart. "I don't like to be angry all the time. And it seems if I'm not mad, I'm sad. My therapist says a lot of it comes from my traumatic childhood."

"Yes. It was difficult," Sarah agreed. "But you're a survivor. The past is history. The only reality is now. You and I sitting here talking together. What happened before you came here tonight is already finished. New adventures are ahead."

"I believe in what you're saying. But in the kind of life-style I lead, it's hard to incorporate a lot of love."

Sarah pulled her robe around her knees. "Then change your life-style. For a while, anyhow."

"How?" Jesseree frowned. "I can't just leave everything I've worked for and go off in another direction. How would I live? Support myself?"'

"Look where you are now." Sarah lifted her palms. "Tonight your emotions are shattered. I believe it's insanity to stay in a situation that's so destructive."

Jesseree thought a moment. "I ended it with Jacob tonight. That's a start."

Sarah nodded. "Good, if that's how you feel. But what about the other aspects of your life?"

Yes. The agency. But she'd worked hard to achieve her position at Kurlay. *You just don't give up a career with a snap of your fingers. One that you've worked so hard to develop.*

"You don't have to give up anything." It was almost like Sarah read Jesseree's mind. "Just get away from it all for a while. Get yourself centered. Then you can make sound decisions."

Get away. Where would she go alone?

"There are wonderful healing retreats in Northern California," Sarah continued. "You could learn to rebuild your life there. You can get the money. You have your inheritance. Call your grandmother. She'll send you what you need."

True. Anytime she needed extra money, her grandmother sent it. In another year-and-a-half, the money would all be hers, anyway. "I'll think about it."

"Let's work on it together," Sarah said. "I'll see what I can do on this end. Between the two of us nothing is impossible."

"I will think about it," Jesseree repeated.

But she felt the wheels had been put in motion. All of her life a magnetic force had bonded her to Sarah. As the two women smiled into each other's eyes, a silent pact was made.

∾∾∾

Jesseree awoke in the morning to the sun streaming through the floor-length windows of Sarah's living room. She stretched and sat up. The room was still. Sarah and Devon must still be sleeping. She pulled up her knee and eyed her foot. Most of the swelling had gone. Gingerly placing both feet on the carpet she stood. With only a slight limp she crossed to the windows and stretched.

Out on the bay, the weekend sailors were already boating .From the hill, their white sails looked like miniature flags slapping the strong winds as they fought to stay afloat. She thought about her parents then shook her head. No time for sad memories. Last night had been enough.

She found paper and pen on Sarah's desk and scribbled a note of thanks. At the bottom of the page she added a note to Devon. She knew he didn't like her. He probably wouldn't care but, because of Sarah's affection for him, Jesseree did the polite thing and thanked him too. After a quick reread, she propped the paper on the fireplace mantle, collected her things, and quietly slipped out the front door.

Sarah's porch overlooked a garden filled with ivy and multi-shades of flowers. Jesseree recalled playing in this garden when she was small. Sarah had told her stories back then of Wee Folk who lived in the yard, gnomes and elves magically existing together in a parallel world.

In the early light, the morning sun filtered through the shrubs and ferns then danced off the moisture gathered on the gray stone sundial. She peered down into the garden, trying to capture a glimpse of the past, but everything in the garden remained still.

She turned and carefully made her way up the dirt path to her car.

Chapter 5

Sarah entered the living room, expecting to find Jesseree still asleep on the sofa, instead she found her note propped behind the incense burner on the mantle. She picked up the paper, squinted, then held it at arm's length. Digging into the pocket of her kimono, she removed reading glasses and pushed them into place. The words jumped into focus and her face relaxed.

When she finished reading, her hand dropped to her side as she gazed out the window at the sailboats on the bay. She wished Jesseree had stayed on a while. Sarah had planned to fix a nice breakfast for her and Devon, hoping they might spend a leisurely morning getting acquainted. A bluebird caught her attention as it dropped from the roof to the garden. The bird jumped up to the sundial where it showered with feathered spasms in the mist. "You're beautiful," she said lovingly, pressing her brow against the glass.

"Who's beautiful?"

Sarah turned quickly. Devon stood behind her. "Good morning, dear." She pointed to the garden. "The bird. It's bathing in the sundial."

Devon went to the windows and his tall figure absorbed the light. He looked for the bird but it had flown away.

She reached out for Devon's hands. "You must be starving. How about breakfast?"

"It's a long drive back to Ahimsa," he said. "I still have preparations to make before my class tomorrow. I must leave soon."

"You have time for tea and a muffin." Sarah scurried up to the kitchen. "Sit down. You have to eat something."

Devon strolled back to the table. "Our visits end too soon. But I'll come back here before long."

When Sarah returned with a tray of food she wondered why he hadn't asked about Jesseree. "Here's a note of thanks from your grateful patient." She held out the paper.

He skimmed over the words with emotionless eyes then handed the note back. "It's good she's feeling better."

"Her foot feels better," Sarah said. "Not her soul. Surely you picked up on her anxiety last night."

Devon stirred his tea. "I did. But then the city's crowded with young women filled with anxiety."

Sarah frowned. "But Jesseree is different. I know this woman. I've watched her grow up. She's ready now for spiritual guidance." She sat down across from him and clasped her hands in her lap. "This girl is like my own child."

"Yes." He nodded thoughtfully. "I can see the love in your eyes."

"She's at a dangerous threshold," Sarah continued. "A life-style change is needed." She broke open a muffin and spread it with butter. "Will you make arrangements for her to stay a few months at Ahimsa?

"What?" Devon lost his Eastern poise. "That would be impossible." He shook his head and looked away.

"It's not impossible."

His eyes darkened as he regained the cool of his mother's ancestors. "You're asking too much. It would be cruel to bring her into the consciousness at Ahimsa. I'd feel responsible for her." He shook his head. "I'm too busy."

"Speak to Sebastian," Sarah persisted. "Call him now. Tell him it's my request."

"It's a hard life in the mountains," Devon reminded her. "Your friend's hands are soft and manicured."

"I didn't say it would be easy for her."

He shook his head again. "She's on a different path."

"No," Sarah argued. "It may look that way to you but

that's not true. She's trying to remove herself from a bad social scene. She's learned all her lessons in that environment. It's time for her to move on."

Devon leaned back and folded his arms. "You could help her just as well as I could."

"You may be right. But it's the change of scene she needs. Besides, she'll respond faster if she's around younger people and has excellent teachers like you and Sebastian."

Devon got up and crossed to the sofa where Jesseree had spent the night. He looked up at the painting of the Himalayas, his gaze settling on the carved head of Buddha resting on a teak wood table below. He hated acting like a spiritual elitist about Sarah's friend.

"Please, Devon. Search your heart. You teach selfless love at the retreat. Use some of your own to help this young woman." She crossed to the door and flung it open. "Come here," she called back. "Just look at this sky. The clouds always hold a message."

He joined her and there was a trilling of unseen birds. Placing an arm affectionately around the older woman's shoulders, he gazed up and nodded.

೧൭೧

Jesseree stepped up to the foyer of the old stucco. Her mailbox was stuffed with paper. She pulled out the paper and shoved it in between her sash and evening bag as she made her way down the hall to her apartment. After bumping the door closed behind her, she plopped her stuff on the kitchen counter and opened the folded papers. Three notes. Two from Jacob and one from Maureen. She pushed Jacob's aside and read Maureen's.

Dear Jess. Worried about you. Phillip and I dropped by your place after the party. Let me know if I can help. Love, Maureen.

Touched by Maureen's concern, she vowed to explain everything to her at the office tomorrow, but right now she needed time to herself. For a long moment, she stared at Jacob's scrawled handwriting before she crumpled the paper and threw it in the trash unread.

A meow at the window alerted her to the neighbor's cat. She smiled at the tiger face pressed against the glass. "Come on, baby." She opened the window. "Come to Jess." The cat pushed into the kitchen with a stiff-legged gait, and arched its back warmly against her velvet pant leg. She picked him up and rubbed her cheek against his soft head as he purred next to her chin.

Sitting down on the window ledge, she rested her back against the sash and gazed at the sky. Silver clouds pushed to the east and she thought about Sarah. When she was a kid, Sarah told her the sky was the blackboard of the universe. As the clouds changed formation, she would read all kinds of fantastic messages to her. Jesseree nodded. What were those old clouds saying today?

Slipping from the windowsill, she crossed to the

cupboard for the cat food she stocked for her friend. After sprinkling a few kibbles on a newspaper, a sudden weariness washed over her and she lowered the window leaving a gap wide enough for the cat to leave. She unplugged the phone and, dropping designer clothes along the way, she headed for the bedroom. Hated to do it, but she carefully cut the seam of her expensive pant leg with a cuticle scissor, and slipped the velvet material over her ankle. With a weary sigh, she climbed under the comforter on her queen- size bed. Cat noiselessly pounced up near her feet and curled into a ball. In two minutes, they were both asleep.

ۍۍۍ

The open room filled with indigo mist that floated around her in rhythmic patterns to the music that spilled from an invisible harp. The warm air was heavy with the scent of Jasmine and dried palm leaves that hung from opaque parapets.

A polished wooden lounge, curved at both ends, held her small reclining figure clad in emerald silk. A gold belt cinched her waist and shifted as she carefully smoothed the folds of gossamer on her rounded hips. She adjusted the silver bracelet entwined around her upper arm as she leaned back on the curved wood and let her long black hair fall over her shoulders.

From the open chamber where she lay, she could see

towering arches and rows of marble columns carved with intricate designs that lined the endless corridors. In the distance, purple-shadowed mountains rose high.

To her right, giant pillars reached up through the mist to the open ceiling where a gateway surrounded by bright light seemed to hold the promise of peace through its portals. So familiar. All so familiar.

A high-pitched flute joined the strains of the harp and the instruments blended magically, stirring her senses with restless yearnings. A man's luminous face emerged from the mist above, his dark head wound with a turban held by an amethyst clasp.

His form expanded then faded with the light that pulsated from the amethyst stone. He reached down and brushed the top of her hair with his fingers and she knew by the depth of his eyes, the purity of his soul. No words passed between them. As the mist shifted around him in a rainbow of pinks and violet, he called to her through the vibrations of the music. Reaching down for her hands, he strove to lift her from the lounge. Her petite body strained to help. The gate began to close and he desperately tried to lift her once more. Tears streamed down her face and her heart ached with the knowledge that they would soon be parted. He hovered above her, reluctant to leave, then his form faded…faded…and was gone.

With one hand, she clutched her breast as she watched him disappear. With the other, her fingers reached out in vain as she sobbed, "Devon—come back!"

                              ∽∾∽

A blast from the outdoor buzzer brought her sharply awake. For a moment, her eyes focused on a beige lampshade on the end table as she tried to identify the noise.

Another blast from the buzzer sent chills down her spine. She knew what it was. Who it was. She turned her head to the wall and frowned. He could buzz his head off for all she cared. She'd be damned if she'd answer. Jacob couldn't get into the foyer without her releasing the latch, yet an unexplained fear clutched her stomach, and she drew her knees to her chest. With a yank, she pulled the quilt up over her head.

He had to know she was home. Her car was parked out in front. She wrapped her arms around her middle then dug her fingers into the hollow of her waist. The buzzer sounded again. Her hands flew up and pressed hard against her ears.

She stayed that way until she was sure he had gone. Slowly, she relaxed her legs and brought her head up for air. By now he was probably down at the corner, trying to call from the booth. Too bad. She'd unplugged her phone.

Her eyes found the lamp again. The lavender color of the ceramic base brought back the strange dream. It had seemed so real—so beautiful—and sad. As the emotions from the dream surged through her again, she envisioned the open room filled with mist. But why had she called that man in her dream Devon? He hadn't looked like Sarah's friend. But she hadn't looked like herself either. Not with that tiny figure and dark hair.

Who knew what her dreams meant? Maybe Paula could figure it out tomorrow. She nodded. Paula would help her work through it. But as she prepared for her bath, the strange feelings from the dream hung on. She brushed her hair vigorously and pinned it high on her head. After testing the water with her toes, she poured in bubbly oil and slid into the comfort of the foam. She leaned back and closed her eyes. The dream's haunting strain played over and over in her head. Once she tried to hum it, but her notes fell flat in the small steam-filled room.

Fifteen minutes later when she lifted her legs from the tub, she tried again, but she couldn't capture the melody. Wrapping herself in a huge green bath towel, she crossed to the vanity and studied her reflection in the oval mirror. Slowly removing the pins from her light hair, she let the strands tumble to her shoulders. With damp fingers, she separated the thick strands then let them fall loose.

She admired the color of the towel against her skin, the same shade as the silk gown in her dream. Good Lord! She laughed out loud. Enough about the silly dream! At least it wasn't frightening like the sinking nightmare she'd been having lately.

Still, she couldn't shake off the sadness of this one—

and the abandoned feeling from the loss of a love.

She tied on a white fleece robe and glanced at the clock on the dresser. Time to call her grandmother. Grandma would be thrilled to hear that she'd spent the night with her old friend, Sarah. But that was all Jesseree intended to tell. No point burdening her with all the gruesome details of her chaotic life.

She plugged in the phone but before she could lift the receiver, it rang. She stiffened. On the fifth ring, she lifted it and shouted, "What do you want?"

There was a pause. "Jesseree—child—what's the matter?"

Jesseree flushed. "Sarah?"

"Yes, dear."

"I'm sorry," Jesseree whispered. "I thought you were Jacob."

Sarah's voice brightened. "Well, I won't keep you but a minute. I just called to tell you I have good news."

Chapter 6

Jacob bolted up the carpeted steps two at a time. Still steaming inside, he stopped at the door to his apartment and searched through his pockets for the keys. Outside the cool weather was typical for San Francisco in September, yet a trickle of sweat ran down the center of his nose.

Damn Jess! He turned his pockets inside out. Her fault his keys were missing. She purposely got him upset. Now he'd be forced to go downstairs and get the manager to open his door. He made an abrupt turn and tripped on his shoelace. Scowling, he glared down. Cheap crappy jogging shoes never stayed tied. He hated them. Hated the color. Jess again. She'd talked him into buying them that weekend they spent in Monterey, convincing him that tan with black trim was in. With a yank, he pulled them off and threw them at his locked door.

"Huh," he snorted and started down the stairs. *She wants out. Great!* He shook his head. *She must think I'm stupid, for God's sake. Her car's parked out in front of her place. I know she's in there.* His eyes narrowed. *But with who? That photographer friend of Maureen's? So what?* Whoever he was, he'd soon wind up a poor bastard. Rejected and alone.

Jacob didn't have proof that Jesseree had seen anyone else since they'd been together, but he always had his suspicions. And now, after she refused earlier to let him in, while he stood outside her place like some desperate idiot with his finger planted firmly on the buzzer, the thought of her unreasonable rejection washed over him, making him sick.

The overweight landlady, uncombed graying hair, still in her flowered robe, followed him up to his apartment, grumbling all the way. She unlocked his door then went on to scold him for disturbing her Sunday TV Movie.

"Stuff it," he muttered and slammed the door in her face.

Inside, he stumbled over a thick law book he'd left on the floor. He kicked it and it flew against the opposite wall with a thud. If Jess cared for him at all, she'd move in here and help him keep this place straight. Fix a meal. Do a load of wash. He had enough stress wearing him down with his studies. Damn it! Was she blind? Couldn't she see he needed help?

She didn't care. Why should she? She had it easy with her trendy clothes, meeting celebrities every day, going to parties. Like last night at Oz. He crumbled into his shoulders, recalling how she'd angrily left and humiliated him. He grabbed the phone and punched in her number. Time now to let her know what a selfish bitch she was. After eleven unanswered rings, he slammed the receiver down and glared at the phone. His mood darkened as he imagined her in bed with some other guy, while he stood here suffering.

He stomped barefoot across the small living room floor and slumped into a chair. A photo of Jesseree beamed a smile from his desk top. He grabbed a pillow from the small of his back and flung it, knocking the picture face down with a crash. "You'll pay for this," he shouted.

Jumping up, he went to the kitchen and mixed a drink. With the bottle tucked under his arm, he came back and sprawled on the sofa. From across the room, the soft colored light and constant rhythm of the bubbling fish tank caught his attention. "Poor babies," he crooned. "You must be hungry. What kind of a daddy am I, anyhow?"

Downing his drink, he wiped his mouth with the back of his hand. A round bowl bright with goldfish sat on the table next to him. Reaching into the bowl he gently scooped up two shining forms and stared at them blankly. He crossed the room to the lighted tank.

Two steely piranhas with orange bellies rose to the surface, eyes bulging with hunger. He fed the unsuspecting wriggling goldfish to their slimy predators. Jacob clicked his tongue with delight. The piranhas gulped their dinner then sank to the bottom of the tank.

"Don't ever do that again," Jess had warned the first time she'd seen him feed his fish. "I'll leave and never come back. It's barbaric! Don't you know those horrible things—those piranhas—are illegal?"

He patted the tank affectionately. That woman had always been unreasonable. These piranhas were his children. He poured another drink and gulped it down. The movement of the water in the tank mesmerized him as the vodka started to hit. He leaned over and switched on the stereo then pushed a pillow behind his head. Memories of happier days flooded his muddled brain and he thought he saw Jess's smiling face floating in the water. Raising his empty glass in a silent toast, he began to cry.

The phone rang. He jumped up and grabbed the receiver. "Jess?"

"No." A pause. "This is your mother."

"Mom," he whined, as tears of frustration stung his eyes. "Jess left me."

Chapter 7

The Sierra Mountains were splashed with Indian Summer color. The strong heat of July and August had passed and the frosty nights had turned the autumn foliage into red and golden earth tones. Only the tall pines remained unchanged. As the forest prepared for winter, the evergreens remained impervious to the weather. Their strong branches would still hold green needles when the heavy snow bent their limbs.

Devon loved all this mountain country but especially the whispering pines. When he listened with his heart to the music the wind played on their boughs and he allowed himself to tune in, his life flowed serenely like a river to the sea.

The beauty of this high country, no matter what time

of year, remained breathtaking, but autumn continued to be his favorite season. He felt more energized at this time of the year. More alive. Tomorrow morning, he would arise at dawn and fill his lungs with the cool life force of this high country.

All afternoon, he'd been driving with the dry air blowing in through the car window. He regretted not stopping and filling his canteen with water ten miles back in Gold Dust. But he hadn't stopped once since he left Sarah's place in Sausalito over four hours ago. Glancing at his watch, he nodded. Tea would soon be served at Ahimsa. He would arrive just in time.

The weekend had been long and exhausting but the lectures and films on world peace had gone well. The Palace of Fine Arts had been packed with people concerned over nuclear war. And not just the younger generation clamored for information on alternative methods for keeping the planet together, now older adults were eager to be enlightened. As more and more people realized that peace could only come about through them, they wanted to learn how. With the knowledge he had gained, he had outlined the beginning of a plan for seekers to follow, but in the future, his dream to help transcribe ancient scrolls recently found in a remote region of Egypt, gave him hope that the truth to global peace lay within the venerated parchments.

The movement of the race toward the Aquarian Age grew steadily and he kept busy, alerting as many of his brothers and sisters as he could. Centers of Light all over the planet were informing nations of the coming disasters and cataclysms that had been predicted by prophets. The message that man must take hold of his destiny and reverse the flow of negative energy was rapidly being circulated.

Usually after productive weekends, his spirit felt exhilarated. But this afternoon as he neared the ashram, he felt tired and angry with himself. The success of the meetings had been rewarding, but last night at Sarah's had left him with a heavy feeling.

This young woman and her problems. What was her name? Jesseree—yes. Just when he had convinced himself that he had let go of the past, a scene like last night made it clear that he hadn't.

His mood darkened matched the filtered shadows of the pines spread across the dirt road. His old rambler rocked and sputtered as it fought its way out of large ruts filled with dried leaves. Each time before he drove to the coast he had his vehicle tuned-up for the trip, but these last few rough miles were always the crucial ones. On this last steep hill, the mass of green metal rebelled. Lifting his foot from the gas pedal, he patted the dusty dash and his dark mood softened. "Just a few more miles, old friend, Then we'll both rest."

His mind drifted back to Jesseree and he scowled. Spoiled. Consumer advocate. He caught himself in midthought. How could he still feel this way about American women? His mother's anger and sorrow must still be buried somewhere deep inside of him. By now, it should have all been erased, but judging by the tension he felt, and his obvious critical behavior last night toward Sarah's friend, he must face the truth about himself.

The ways of the West had been difficult for his mother. She had never really adjusted. Perhaps she didn't try. He recalled his feelings of embarrassment as a child when she came to his school dressed in her native saris. The Holy City of Varanasi, where she had been born, was famous for its silk weaving factory and his mother had worked there as a girl. When she got older, she taught the secret of draping the classic sari to the tourists. He remembered how, in this country, her eyes shone with pride each time she draped her rich silks about her rounded figure. Even at the early age of eight, he'd been aware of his mother's discontent. One afternoon when he returned from school, he found her softly crying under the eucalyptus tree in their small back yard.

"Mother, what's wrong?" he had cried, putting his young arms around her neck.

She had looked up at him sadly, her round dark eyes full of tears. "My baby," she said in her native tongue. "It is nothing—do not worry your head—it is just that everything and everyone here is so strange."

"Mother," he had pleaded. "Speak English."

She released him as she wiped her eyes with her fingertips and became silent.

The years passed and she seemed to settle for her new life. The loneliness for her family and country was seldom voiced, and eventually she became involved with other women in the neighborhood. Her life became busy as she buried herself in community projects, until one terrible day years later when he arrived home after his classes at the university.

His mother, the quiet Eastern beauty, had erupted. She had just learned of his father's love for an American woman, and she was immersed in a cloud of hate. She clutched wrinkled blue stationary wet from her stormy tears in her trembling fingers. "They are all the same, my son," she cried. "Greedy and wanton. The West will destroy you with its grasping ways. Come back with me to the home of our cradle," she pleaded, her head bent to the side in a gesture of grief. "We will be with our own near the Ganges."

The Ganges! No! He was home. The United States had been home since he turned twelve. His veins surged with the blood of the West as well as the East. "Mother," he said. "Please. Tell me what happened."

But she refused to give him details. Like a madwoman, she stormed through the house packing her bags. After hours of trying to reason with her, and when he was positive she really meant to leave, he sat down quietly. "I can't go with you. My heart follows you but my studies are here. Perhaps someday I will return but not now."

His mother's tears turned to sobs. Soon threats of

doom escaped from her choked voice. "Then live with these foreigners, Devon. They will destroy you as they have destroyed me." She buried her face in her hands and when she looked up again her mouth tightened and her black eyes filled with pain. "Your father will desert you—I swear. If you stay in this country, you will suffer."

Devon remained firm. "I love you mother." He tried to reassure her. "But if you choose to return to your home, you will do so without me."

When she sailed for India, despair and sorrow plagued him for months. A growing resentment toward his father affected his studies. But he couldn't bring himself to question his dad about the other woman. His father didn't offer an explanation and Devon didn't ask. Instead he moved out and into a room near his school.

For months he studied books of theology as he tried to work his way through his loneliness. Finally after long nights of reading, he came to the realization that in love there is no separation. He found an English translation of the Bhagavad Gita, the Hindu philosophical book, and for the first time, he really understood the ancient words, "thine own duty born of thine own nature."

A new group formed on the campus of UC Berkeley and he joined them. They were followers of the Gandhi Sutras in the early seventies and the non-violence theology strongly appealed to him after the frightening protests and sit-ins against the Vietnam War. As far back as he could recall, even as a child in India, violence was never a part of his nature—but then—if that were true, how could he explain his attitude now about Sarah's friend? His anger? Emotional violence?

He sighed deeply. He still had much work ahead to release old patterns. At least he was aware of them. If he truly believed what he taught, then he must eventually come to view Jesseree as a perfect creation of the universe.

But right now he was having problems with that concept. He couldn't foresee a lengthy stay for her at the ashram. Through the years, he'd watched people come and go. Curiosity about life on the outside had lured most of them away. In his opinion that would be the pattern for Jesseree.

He did hope that Sarah had made it clear to her that Ahimsa was not an escape from life, and she would bring her problems along with her. And if she didn't have some creative interest to sustain her, she could wind up a useless daydreamer.

He shook his head in an effort to dismiss negative thoughts. After these trips to the city, he struggled to get centered again. This slipping back into instant judgment, or any judgment at all, was something he had been fighting daily.

He pressed the washer button on the dash and a thin stream of water hit the windshield. The wipers moaned as they scraped the red dust into rivulets. Within seconds the glass cleared and, when he peered through the fan-shaped brightness, he could see the beauty of the trees once more. It felt good to return to teaching and his studies. His spiritual battery needed recharging. And if Jesseree decided to come to Ahimsa, he must believe that it was cosmic order.

The entrance to the retreat rose up suddenly when he turned the final curve. A wooden sign hung from a chain that spanned two tall poles. The sign read *AHIMSA*. Below, deeply chiseled in the wood, *A HERMITAGE OF SELFLESS LOVE*.

Devon pulled on the hand brake. He reread the words and remembered that hot summer morning when the posts were set and pointed toward the sky. What a joyous celebration as a handful on new Gandhi disciples committed their lives toward world peace. They had all stood in a circle holding hands as they offered thanks for the wilderness property that had so miraculously come into their keeping.

Now eleven year later, they were almost a self-sustaining community and their dedication had strengthened them tremendously. The mortgage on the land would be paid in less than two months. They had done well.

A brisk breeze blew up, pushing the sign to and fro in an off-centered swing. He watched until the wind passed and the wood hung still. That's what he needed— to calm himself against the passing winds of judgment.

To regain his balance. Tomorrow, he had students waiting to learn about selfless love and peace. He would be
their teacher.

Farther up the hill, a tinkle of bells called for evening
meditation. Time to be still and know. He eased the dusty
car through the pole entrance and left the turmoil of the
city behind.

Chapter 8

Jesseree leaned against the reception desk at Kurlay and compulsively counted the gold stripes on the rust carpet as she waited for Maureen to get off the phone.

"Okay, what's happening?" Maureen offered as she hung up.

"I'm leaving for the mountains. I just wanted to see you before things got too hectic in here. And Maureen—" Jesseree's voice shook. "Please. Please—no matter what he says or does—"

"Whoa. Wait a minute. Settle down." Maureen stood and made her way around to the front of her desk. "How about some coffee?"

"No," Jesseree shook her head. "I don't have time. I just want to get out of this city."

Maureen squinted in disbelief. "For good?"

Jesseree collapsed into a red leather chair. "No. I'll be back. But right now I need to get some distance between me and everything—and everyone. It's now or never."

Maureen poured coffee into a mug and handed it to her. "Here. Sip on this." At her desk she pulled a quart thermos from the middle drawer and poured orange juice into a paper cup. "You look awful."

Jesseree frowned. "I don't need the criticism."

"I'm sorry. I didn't mean—I'm only trying to—" She moved behind the chair and placed her hands on Jesseree's shoulders and began kneading with her fingers.

Jesseree straightened. Grasping the steaming mug, she rolled her head slowly while Maureen massaged out the knots. "That feels great. Just what I need."

"Okay. Now let's have it. Why are you leaving for the mountains on a Monday morning?"

Jesseree placed the cup on the table next to the juice. "Because I'm taking a leave of absence. Mr. Crandall thinks I need a rest. I talked to him about this last night." She closed her eyes and grimaced when Maureen hit on a tight muscle in her neck.

"So when will you be back?"

"I promised Crandall I'd return by the first of the year for the Moody Contract." Jesseree slid forward in the chair and turned to face Maureen. "Just don't tell Jacob where I am or what I'm doing. Or when I'm coming back."

"Is he why you're leaving?"

"Partly." Jesseree made a broad sweep with both arms. "And because of my whole screwed up life."

Maureen clasped Jesseree's hands. "I'm going to miss you, gal. You're the only authentic person around this place."

Jesseree stood and rotated her shoulders before she took a gulp of the juice. "I'll miss you too but I've got to go."

"Can't you tell me where? And what about your apartment? Should I have the key?"

"That's been taken care of. Cheryl's staying there. She has to drop a couple of pounds for the Pepsi commercials and she can't do it and live with junk-food Don." Jesseree grabbed for her bag. "It's all working out. Everything's falling into place."

Maureen shook her head impatiently. "Will you please tell me where you're going or what?"

"Not right now. Hey! I don't even know if I'll stay where I'm headed. But if I do, I promise I'll drop you a card. If there's a phone, I'll call. I will keep in touch." Jesseree glanced over at Maureen with a panic look. "Just don't tell Jacob anything."

The two women embraced and Maureen held on to her, reluctant to let go.

"I'm serious about Jacob not knowing anything about me. I'm scared of him. He's been acting weird." Jesseree folded her arms and shook her head. "He drinks all the time and now he's using."

"Using what?"

"He's snorting."

Maureen searched her face. "That's not unusual, Jess. There's a lot of—"

"I don't care about a lot of other people," Jesseree interrupted. "I'm not dating a druggie."

"Okay." Maureen stepped back, holding up her palms. "If Jacob is wrinkling your pretty skin, then get out. I'll help any way I can."

Jesseree hugged her again and her eyes were moist. She glanced in the mirror above the desk and winced. "You're right. I look a mess." She ran her fingers through her hair then slipped on her dark glasses. "Better get out of here before somebody comes in." She started for the door. "One more thing." She reached in her bag and removed a card. "I have a friend in Sausalito. I'm leaving her number with you. If you haven't heard from me and something important—a crisis—well, call her. Sarah Brunson. She'll know where to find me."

The phone rang. Maureen turned to answer as Jesseree closed the office door behind her.

Out on Sutter Street, the sun flooded her face. Autumn, the most beautiful time of the year in the city for tourists and she was leaving it all behind.

When she was a kid, her grandmother took her for rides on the cable cars during tourist season. Grandma had a regal flair dressed in a hat and gloves. Before they took the cable car to Aquatic Park, there would be a ritual stop at Blums for hot fudge sundaes.

But San Francisco was different now. Changed. Some good, some bad. As she strolled down the sidewalk, she spotted a phone booth across the street and made a dash for the other side. Halfway across, a sharp twinge from her sore ankle caused her to stumble.

"Move it," a driver hung out his window and hollered while he honked and pointed at the light.

She pulled her sweater tightly around her, adjusted her dark glasses, and hurried across. At the booth, she dialed Sarah's number.

"Hi. I'm leaving now, Sarah. Just wanted to check in before I go." The receiver felt cold against her cheek.

"That's fine, dear. Your voice sounds a bit shaky. Are you feeling all right?"

"Yes I'm okay—a little nervous. I don't know what to expect." She paused and took a deep breath. "I'll call you when I get settled. I left your number with Maureen, the receptionist at Kurlay. She's a friend."

A frowning, middle-aged woman tapped insistently on the glass behind her. Jesseree peered around. "I'll be through here in a minute."

The woman muttered something foreign then set her shopping bags down with a thud.

"What's happening there? Is someone with you?"

"No. No. Just a woman impatiently waiting outside of the booth."

"All right then, dear, I'll let you be on your way, Remember my heart goes with you."

Good. I'm off then. First to the bank. I'm having my checks sent to the retreat. Then I'll hit the road. I love you."

She hung up and sighed. When things settled down, she'd make a point to call Sarah at least once a week. As she stepped from the booth, the waiting woman almost knocked her off balance as she hipped her way into the cubicle. Jesseree felt like saying something nasty but instead she took a deep breath and looked up toward the sky.

Across the street above a building rose a billboard. Her own face smiled back at her. In the ad, she lay on her side wearing a black satin dress and holding a martini glass in her bright tipped fingers. Her light hair tumbled across one bare shoulder, subliminally suggesting to the male population that if they bought her brand of vodka they might get her for a nightcap.

Sick! The whole damn advertising strategy. She studied her face in the big picture. Wow! Didn't she look perfect up there, holding the whole world in the palm of her hand? If she'd told that woman waiting for the phone that she was the model on the billboard, she probably would have scoffed in her face.

Jesseree recalled when they did that shoot they had to physically lower her onto that fur mat and fluff it up around her elbows. When they were through shooting, they had to lift her to her feet. That dress had been so skin tight she couldn't move. She could still hear the photographer screaming, "Don't rip that gown. For God's sake, she's getting wrinkled."

Jesseree sighed deeply, turned, and walked away. Minutes later, as she pulled from the downtown parking garage, a chorus of voices rang out. She turned to look as a wave of peace marchers spanned the street carrying banners. *FREEZE THE ARMS RACE—BILLIONS SPENT FOR DEFENSE WHILE MILLIONS ARE HOMELESS.*

She switched off the motor and rolled down the window. The marchers strode along the street, arm in arm, holding back the early traffic. As they approached the corner, their strong voices pealed out: "Gonna lay down my sword and shield, down by the riverside." They were headed toward the bay. When they passed by her car, Jesseree felt a spurt of positive energy. She longed to join them, be part of something meaningful, but right now she had her own inward battle to fight.

Curious people lined the curbs. Some cheered. Others rushed out to join the marchers. Others, like herself, too busy with their own affairs, hurried off in another direction.

She switched on the ignition and hummed along as

the marchers finished their song and began to chant, "All we are saying is give peace a chance."

She turned the corner, vowing that when she returned to San Francisco, stronger in spirit, she would join them too.

Glancing back at the billboard, she shook her head and murmured, "Sure as hell beats that."

Chapter 9

The road up through the Sierra became steep and winding and, because she was unaccustomed to mountain roads, Jesseree rode her brake on every curve. At one point the highway narrowed dangerously into a one-lane with a sign *DUE TO FLOODING* posted on the side. Jesseree slowed down to a crawl.

As she approached the old gold mining town of Downieville, dark clouds from the north gathered in, blocking out the sun that had followed her in from San Francisco. The gray masses swirled, merged, then hung like a dark sheet above the small town carved out of the canyon.

Sarah's map lay on the seat beside her. Jesseree leaned over and checked it once more as she entered the main street that paralleled the Yuba River. Had she missed the cutoff? Holding the map across the steering wheel, she slowed, pulled into a parking area next to the grocery store, and stepped out. A strong wind tore off the loose scarf draped around her neck. She chased after it and bumped into an old man dressed in dusty clothes crossing the street.

She reached out and supported his arm. "I'm sorry."

The old man grinned, flashing two gold teeth. "You didn't break nothin'." His tanned and weathered skin held deep creases around his eyes that turned to white lines when his face sobered. "Just visiting, are you?"

"No, not visiting. Passing through." Jesseree glanced around uncertainly. "But I don't know if... Well, it looks like I'm lost."

"Where you headed?

"I have a map in my car. Could you help me, please?"

He nodded and followed. She placed the road map on the hood of her car then positioned Sarah's printed one on top. "I'm looking for Ahimsa. Do you know where that is?"

The old man looked puzzled as he leaned heavily against the fender.

Jesseree studied the maps. "These two maps don't seem to coincide."

The old timer squinted. "Don't what?"

"See?" Jesseree pointed. "This road map shows I've

still got a way to go. But this other one says—" Jesseree
shrugged. "I'm probably not reading it right."

The old timer's nose almost touched the paper. "I
can't see without my specs." His mouth smiled but his
eyes turned cold. "Name of the place again? What did
you call it?"

"Ahimsa. It's a retreat. The map says to turn left on
Glory Road."

The man spat over his shoulder. The wet brown plug
hit the dirt, cratering the loose soil. "That's where those
peace preachers live, ain't it?"

Jesseree laughed. "Peace what?"

"They think they can stop the bombs with their meetings. Lord, they don't even know what war's about." He
spat again licking his puffy lips with the tip of his coated
tongue. "Fought in the big one myself."

He rolled up a flannel sleeve and rubbed a spot just
below his elbow. "Still got the scar. Hit with shrapnel."

Jesseree frowned. "I'm sorry you were wounded."

"Don't hurt anymore." He rolled the sleeve back
down and buttoned it at the wrist with stiff fingers. "Are
you in a hurry?"

"Kind of. I want to get there before it gets too late.
And I don't know if I'm headed in the right direction."

"You ain't." The man smiled, his eyes lighting up
with mischief. "It's back about eight miles." He studied
her face. "Say. What's a pretty one like you going up
there for?"

Jesseree shrugged.

When she didn't answer, he pointed a gnarled finger toward the hill behind her and drew a curve in the air. "Turn around and go back until you see the third dirt road on your right." "Shouldn't take you that long."

"Good," she said, relieved. "Thanks for your help."

The old man shuffled toward the store and spat brown again.

"Have a nice day," she called after him.

He stopped and waved. "If it gets too boring up there, come on back and I'll tell you some real stories about the big one." He grabbed the corner of the building and pulled himself up the wooden steps to the boardwalk. "Them young ones," he muttered. "Don't know what the hell war's all about."

Jesseree gathered up the maps and tossed them into the car. The wind blew her hair and she tied the silk scarf around her head. The scarf had been a gift from Jacob the weekend they spent together in Monterey. It was an unusual paisley print in wheat and gold. "Matches your hair," he had said as he placed it around her shoulders.

Jacob did have nice taste in some things.

A sign across the road heralded homemade sandwiches. Except for the coffee and juice Maureen had fixed for her earlier at Kurlay, she hadn't eaten all day.

After she got her order, she took her avocado sandwich outside to a redwood table and bench under a closed umbrella near the river. The river, reflecting gray from the overcast sky, tumbled lazily over washed boulders. When the tired-eyed waitress, with short brown hair, brought out the check, Jesseree left the soothing sounds of the river and reluctantly headed back to the car.

On her right, a worn metal bridge spanned the river. Instead of heading back to her car, she changed her mind and crossed over the bridge. A sudden wind blew up and whipped at her back. She dug her hands deep into the pockets of her sweater as autumn-colored leaves twirled about her legs.

Screened by ominous looking clouds, the silver sun hung low in the sky. She glanced around at the deserted street, guessing the cold wind had shooed folks inside. Half-way across the old bridge, she paused to look over the railing at the now rushing water below tossing leaves and branches to the quieter pools near the banks. Strange. She frowned. How quickly the river had taken a turn.

She continued on across until she stepped from the bridge onto a dirt path. In that instant, the wind stopped. The air grew deathly still. She looked up and the clouds had disappeared, the sun had vanished, yet she stood in bright light. The energy from the light lifted her so that her feet barely touched the ground as she twisted and turned, in slow motion, down the narrow path to a clearing where a scaffold stood.

The surrounding hills were now barren, dotted with sparse and spindly young pine. So unlike the dense forests on those same hills when she entered the town.

Off somewhere, she could hear the beat of a drum.

Ta rum, rum, rum—ta rum, rum, rum.

A scene appeared before her. She gasped and pressed her palm over her heart.

To her right, six pallbearers in dark suits and brimmed hats struggled with a pine coffin covered with fresh yellow flowers. Three women wearing black bonnets and long black dresses followed close behind, wailing and crying.

Ta rum, rum, rum.

On the far left, a weathered wooden gallows supported dark figures preparing an execution. One hooded shadow placed a knotted noose over the head of a young man in a dingy white shirt, denim trousers, and dusty brown boots, while a sea of curious faces swirled and swayed below.

Ta rum, rum, rum.

The funeral procession drew near, headed for the crossing at the bridge. Red dust rose up from the dry earth, clinging to the plain black clothes of the mourners as their feet dragged along to the beat. Ta rum, rum, rum.

"My son—oh, my son," the middle woman wept. "Dear Lord, why?"

Her head fell back and, from beneath the bonnet, Jesseree could see her tear stained face.

Sarah! Good Lord, it was Sarah!

From high on the scaffold, the gallows trap sprung open. With horror, Jesseree watched as the young man dropped to his death. A girl in her late teens screamed and fainted. A man from the crowd rushed to her side to support her head. He removed a scarf from around her neck, dampened it with water from his canteen and laid it across her forehead. Jesseree inched closer. The man placed the canteen to the girl's lips and Jesseree recognized the dampened scarf. It was paisley print in wheat and gold. Her scarf! The same color as the young girl's hair.

Jesseree slapped her hands over her eyes and screamed. As the sound reverberated around the empty hills, her ears rang with the terror of her own voice. She tried to run back to the bridge, but she was forced along in another direction by the bright light that surrounded her toward a log courthouse that stood behind the scaffold. There the force let go and she dropped onto a wooden bench. Shaken, she placed her hands on the chipped planks and gripped the sides for support.

Her fingers crumpled a newspaper lying beside her on the bench. When she looked down at the historic print, the paper was dated, September 25, 1885.

The pallbearers had moved on and neared the bridge. In desperation, Jesseree struggled to her feet. "Sarah," she called after them. "Sarah—wait."

Ta rum, rum, rum.

Her calls unheeded, the procession continued on. As they entered a covered bridge, she caught up with them.

She took one step up on the wood and the covered

bridge was suddenly metal again. No funeral procession ahead of her. No beat of a drum. The bright light slowly faded around her. When she looked up, the dark clouds lay overhead like a shroud. Once again, the surrounding hills were crowded with thick pines, and the strong winds of before tore at her sweater and whipped at the scarf tied around her head.

She blinked and fell to her knees, covering her face with her hands. Huge sobs shook her body as the wind howled down from the canyon like the moans from the women in that distant place. Jesseree remained kneeling, rocking and crying for what seemed an eternity.

When she finally got hold of herself and stood, she looked back. The weathered gallows in the clearing still stood silhouetted against the forested mountains in a mocking reminder of the horror of the past.

She rummaged through her bag until she found her Valium. She held up the container and stared blankly at the prescription. With shaking fingers, she removed the plastic lid and emptied the yellow tablets into the rushing river below. Letting the plastic bottle slip from her hand, she watched as it bobbed along and disappeared into the rapids.

"Dear God," she cried out. "What's happening to me?"

Chapter 10

Shirley Kelso's son didn't look well. Something about his eyes. He had been with her since last evening and, usually when he visited, she could count on him being talkative to the extreme. Now he hadn't spoken more than half a dozen words. So unlike him. "Something wrong, Jacob?" she finally asked.

Across the table, Jacob hid behind the morning paper, walling out his mother's face.

Shirley finished breakfast and felt her son would be more than relieved if she left the room. And she planned to leave shortly, but not yet. "Aren't you going to your class today? It is Monday."

Yes. He knew it was Monday—and tomorrow would be Tuesday, but he had no intention of attending classes.

On this particular day, since the sun shone in Marin, he planned to enjoy the day and swim in his parent's pool. Try to enjoy, anyway. All night, he had experienced a sad, dull ache in his groin. What he really wanted? Jess to be here with him.

"Jacob. Talk to me," Shirley pleaded. "All this silence can't be over this girl leaving you. If you're physically ill, just say so, and I'll call Dr. Lepstien. But don't miss your important class."

Jacob dropped the paper across his plate and glared. His mother's pinched face made him uncomfortable. How could she ever understand what Jess meant to him? Now, the realization settled in—Jess would never know either, because he couldn't tell her. Because she wouldn't see him. He stared across the table. If there was anything physically wrong with him, it was because of his mother nosing into his affairs all the time.

He finally spoke. "Why can't I stay here without having this conversation?"

Relieved that at last they were talking, she offered, "You can. But I think an explanation would be nice— maybe later when you feel like it. At least something I can tell your father when he comes home. You know he's sure to ask."

Jacob was Shirley's youngest child, her second son, and this morning she felt full of parental concern for him. She had tried very hard not to keep him tied to her apron strings, but she did want him to know that she deeply cared when he was in trouble. She had made the mistake with her oldest son of holding on too tight and the repercussions had been tremendous. A practicing dentist now living on the East Coast, married to a hygienist, Shirley was lucky to hear from him twice a year. If she wanted to see her only granddaughter, it was up to her to fly to New York. Even then she didn't feel especially welcome. It had been a struggle for her not to make the same mistake with Jacob.

"Is it about school, dear?" She tried once more, searching his face now that he'd removed the morning newspaper from between them. "Is there some problem there?"

"It's always school, dear," Jacob said mockingly. "Is that the only thing that's important to you? If I make it through law school or not?"

Shirley felt the blood rise to her neck. "It is when you're father is paying for it." She bit the inside of her cheek. Not another scene. Not again. She fought to control the shakiness that was suddenly shredding her apart. "I may as well tell you, Jacob, your father's getting tired of your problems. He's threatening to cut your tuition and your allowance if you don't pull it together."

Jacob jumped up, his face red. "Why don't you two butt out of my life? I'm old enough to handle my own affairs."

"Then why don't you do it?" Shirley's eyes blazed at his ungratefulness. "You're old enough but, apparently, not mature enough." Her head throbbed as she nervously rearranged the silverware on the white tablecloth. "We want you to be successful. Capable of taking care of yourself. Independent. Is that too much to ask?"

"Yes!" Jacob screamed. "Stop pressuring me."

He got up and stormed over to the slider door. Grabbing the handle, he threw it open. He hesitated while he stared out. The sparkle of the pool beckoned him on. If he submerged himself in the water maybe, hopefully, it would soak the hurt from his bones and wash the heat from his mind.

Shirley's vision blurred. For a moment she saw a dark-haired boy in cords waving goodbye, throwing her a kiss as he left through that same slider on his way to elementary school.

Was it that long ago? Jacob. She longed to hold him and smooth away his troubles as she had when he was small. Was it too late now?

Her anger subsided. She whispered, "I love you son."

Jacob turned and looked back before he bounded down the brick steps to the pool.

She got up from the table and slowly made her way over to the bar where she poured herself a strong one. Staring into the glass, tears streamed from her eyes. She gulped the drink. With trembling fingers, she set the empty glass down.

"I love you, Jacob," she called after him. Her voice faded. "And so does Dad."

Chapter 11

Jesseree entered the main office at Ahimsa, feeling drained and uneasy.

"Hello there," a man said, greeting her distractedly. "Can I be of assistance?"

Jesseree quickly turned around. It was so quiet in the room she thought it must be empty. "Hello. You can, as a matter-of-fact. I'm Jesseree Lipton from San Francisco. I'll be staying here for a while."

The middle-aged man smiled a warm welcome.

She moved toward his desk uncertainly, child-like, wrapped in her sweater and head scarf, feeling cold and unsure of herself, still shaken from her horrifying experience in Downieville. "I believe arrangements were made by my friend. I should have a reservation."

She could tell by his expression that her name didn't register with him. "Sit down, please." He held out his hand. "I'm, Sebastian, director here at Ahimsa. Your name again? I'm sorry."

She placed her hand in his big tanned one and she immediately felt his warmth. "Sarah Brunson—"

A bright smile spread across his face. "Ah, yes, Sarah," he nodded. "Now I remember. Devon spoke to me about you this morning."

Good grief, Devon! What had he told this director? "I'm really not Devon's friend," she quickly explained. "We have a mutual friend, Sarah."

"We're all friends at Ahimsa, Jesseree. If Devon prepares space for you here, for personal development, then perhaps he is the best friend you will ever know in this lifetime." He smiled with affection. "But first we have a form to fill out then we'll get you settled.

Jesseree sat down in the wicker chair Sebastian held for her. He was a nice looking man. Fiftyish, maybe. His pale blue cotton pants and shirt enhanced the gray streaks in his dark hair.

While he shuffled through the papers on his desk, Jesseree studied the room. Her eyes focused on a plaque hanging on the wall behind his head. *STRENGTH DOES NOT COME FROM PHYSICAL CAPACITY. IT COMES FROM AN INDOMITABLE WILL. ~ Mahatma Gandhi.*

An indomitable will. Exactly what she needed.

The office, filled with books and a few odd pieces of

furniture, had a large braided rug that looked handmade spread across the hardwood floor extending beneath an oil heater in the far corner. On top of the heater, a potted plant with large shiny leaves climbed up a stove pipe that pushed through the rough beamed ceiling.

Posters lined three walls. The water color prints done in unusual colors looked professional. The mountain scenes appeared to be the Sierra, but instead of the standard earth tones, the artist had used various shades of pink and violet.

Below the posters on a narrow table pressed against the wall were framed photos of Gandhi at various stages of his life. Thin pamphlets of sutras were scattered near the edge of the tabletop and a white sign offered: *Please take one*.

Directly behind the table on the brightly painted yellow windowsill stood two small statues. A ceramic Mary dressed in blue and an ivory Kwan Yin. Above them in a gilded frame shone the face of Jesus.

They don't take any chances here, she thought. They've included everyone.

"You mentioned personal development." She interrupted Sebastian's search. "Is this a religious retreat?"

Sebastian looked up. "That depends. How do you define religious?"

Jesseree thought a moment. "I guess I'm wondering about your affiliation."

He slid the drawer closed then placed the paper he

had been searching for on the desk. Leaning back in his chair, he pyramided his fingers. "We try to uphold all spirituality here, acknowledging all forms of life as the One." He smiled reassuringly. "But you will soon see. After you've been here a while it will become clear. I have a theory that if you didn't already know most of this, you wouldn't be here now."

Jesseree didn't understand his theory, but she returned his smile.

They both turned as the door opened. Devon and a pretty young woman with one long braid in her dark hair entered. The woman, dressed in a tan blouse and brown wraparound skirt, wore black cloth shoes secured at the sides with silver buckles.

Sebastian stood. "Come in. We were just talking about you, Devon."

Devon came over, nodded a greeting to Sebastian, then turned to Jesseree. "I hope you had a pleasant trip, Ms. Lipton."

"So formal. Thanks. The drive here was beautiful. And my name is Jesseree. Just call me Jess."

"Of course. And this is Anasuya."

The young woman smiled and took hold of Jesseree's hands. "You can call me Ana." She laughed and her voice tinkled like a bell.

Jesseree loosened the scarf from under her chin and it dropped to her shoulders. Devon watched with genuine interest as she tucked it into the collar of her sweater.

"Jess." Sebastian handed her the paper. "You can fill this out later at the cabin. We have a few rules here. I'm sure you won't have any problem with them. Now I think it's time that Devon and Ana showed you around before it gets too late."

Jesseree stood up next to Devon, a head taller than she. Looking at him closely now for the first time, she was fascinated by the color of his eyes. How striking. Light eyes and dark skin, both eyes and skin clear like a child's. He faced the window and his eyes reflected the afternoon light. They were blue—no, green. Closer to the color of the sea. At Sarah's that first night in the firelight, she could have sworn his eyes were dark. She gazed at them now until he turned away.

"I'm sorry, Ms. Jesseree, but I must leave now."

"Call me Jess."

"I prefer to use Jesseree," he said. "It would be a pity to shorten it. That would change the meaning."

She felt herself blush. "I wasn't aware my name had a special meaning."

Devon looked past her to the clock on the wall. "I really must go. There's gardening to be done." He crossed to the open door where he turned and nodded to the trio. "I'll be joining you at dinner."

Anasuya took Jesseree's arm. "Come on. I'll help unload your car. I have a cabin all set up for you. Did you bring a sleeping bag? We have plenty of blankets but this time of the year, it freezes at night."

The two women left the office arm in arm. Sebastian smiled knowingly as they chattered on like all the other busy creatures who lived in the surrounding woods.

Devon sauntered down the dirt path that led to the vegetable garden—a busy path swept clean of leaves and lined with chunks of quartz rock. Getting to the garden had been an excuse to leave Sebastian's office. When Jesseree had stood next to him, disturbing thoughts had churned around in his head. She stood tall. Surprisingly so. At Sarah's on the sofa he thought of her as a small woman.

He'd made a fool of himself by commenting on her name and then making a swift exit. Jesseree—Jesseree. Someday, when he felt more controlled in her presence, he would tell her the meaning of her name.

He hadn't expected her to arrive so soon. Not today. He wasn't prepared. Ridiculous. Prepared for what? He hoped it was clear to everyone in the office that he was too busy to be her sponsor. Not that Sebastian had hinted that he should, but the responsibility for a newcomer usually rested with the referring member. Him.

Ana seemed drawn to Jesseree. Good. Perhaps the contrast of their personalities would create a nice balance. He must remember that Jesseree had come here not only to learn, but to teach them all as well. What they would learn remained to be seen—or heard.

That night at Sarah's, Jesseree had certainly stirred up emotions that he thought were long gone. Her presence here would be a daily reminder of the work he still needed to do on himself. He dreaded sorting through the old sorrow and pain again, but if he chose to be free of his bitterness, that might be necessary.

Avoiding her was not the answer. True, they would be involved in separate areas of work, but at times they were certain to meet. Ahimsa included twenty acres, but the retreat was where they all lived. He shook his head despairingly. No. He didn't have to take measures to avoid her. He sighed with sudden insight. He didn't have to plan a thing. His soul would lead him to the lessons he must learn.

He sighed again, deeply this time. The spiritual mission he had chosen for himself could not be embarked upon now. Not even if he was accepted. He couldn't leave Ahimsa until these tight emotional knots in his heart were loosened and smoothed out. May as well relax, old fellow, he told his ego. This won't be easy.

"Devon. Over here." Paul waved his short handled hoe in the air. "Look at these tomatoes. Can you believe they're still ripening? He scooted around. "And look. More squash."

Tomatoes growing up here, Devon thought. That is a miracle. When they started the garden years ago, doomsayers predicted that it could never be done. The altitude's too high. Nights get too cold. You're fools if you try.

Well, they were wrong. The garden had flourished

from the start. Since Paul had joined the retreat, he now harvested huge tasty tomatoes long into the fall. And his beets—the size of large pinecones. Paul's vegies! He provided fresh food for everyone until the frosts came. The canned and dried foods prepared from the garden were brought out during the winter.

Paul had a definite feeling for plants. His idea of blocking off a section of the half-acre garden to work in the French Intensive Method had been developed successfully. With the help of the others, he had built timber-lined raised beds where the structure and the fertility of the soil could be adjusted to each plant.

He had also designed wide paths for himself between the raised beds, making it easier for him to move around. This year, his corner of the garden had doubled its productivity.

Paul had come to Ahimsa, like Jesseree and so many other confused souls, seeking answers to problems. He had come searching for ways to cope with his sorrowful life. But two years ago, he had chosen to stay and work to help build the peace consciousness of Ahimsa. The heart of the retreat.

"It's almost a shame to pull up these carrots and beets, isn't it?" he commented, interrupting Devon's thoughts. "Harvesting kills them," Paul continued, rubbing his dirt-streaked face with his glove.

Paul had fought in Vietnam. In Country. Involved in killing. When they'd first met, Sebastian had placed him with Devon. During the first three months of his stay, Devon would wake up to Paul's screaming night terrors. Many nights, sleep became impossible for both of them.

In the beginning, Paul's eyes were wells of sorrow as he audited the lectures at the ashram. In time, he attended meditation classes. Meditation seemed to be the turnaround for him. The nightmares lessened and his hands grew steady. Now, two years later, his face glowed with enthusiasm as he worked on present issues rather than reliving the horrors of the past.

No one fought for world peace harder than Paul. He lectured at high schools and churches all over northern California, convincing young men and women of the futility of war.

Now, Devon watched as Paul poked around the soil with his thick glove. "I know we have to eat something. I bless each life root as I pull it."

Devon nodded and folded his arms. "You're absolutely right. We do have to eat."

Paul looked up. "Thanks for putting the new handle on my hoe. Sometimes I put too much weight on these tools and they break. It's easy to do when you're down here so close to the ground."

"Okay, Paul. It's getting late. Let's go back for evening meditation." Devon grasped the handles of a metal chair and wheeled it over. Leaning over, he helped Paul from his wheeled board, custom made for his chores. Paul reached back and grabbed hold of the arms of the chair. With Devon's help, he raised his legless trunk up onto the cushioned chair and strapped himself in.

Chapter 12

The next morning, a light tapping at the cabin door momentarily aroused Jesseree but she quickly fell back to sleep. The long drive yesterday and all the excitement of getting settled, plus the shocking incident at Downieville had left her exhausted. Last evening, instead of going to the main house for dinner, she'd opted to stay at the cabin and unpack a few things to get settled.

After she finished, she dropped onto the bed into a tunnel of silence from which now she was reluctant to leave.

The tapping at the door grew stronger. She rolled from her stomach to her side, groaning as she stretched her stiff legs against the hard mattress. Opening one eye, she adjusted her vision to the dim light before she could distinguish outlines of the sparse furniture.

"Jess. Jesseree. It's Anasuya. Are you awake?"

Jesseree sat up and looked around the room. Cold— freezing. She fumbled for her robe at the foot of the bed then remembered she had it on. Sometime during the night she must have wrapped it around her shoulders and managed to slip one arm in a sleeve.

"Jess." Anasuya called again. "Can I come in?"

"Sure." Jesseree struggled to get her other arm in the robe while she searched under the bed for her slippers. At least her feet were warm. She had slept in her socks.

Anasuya silently opened the door and peered in. "Good morning. Am I disturbing you?"

Lord, no, Jesseree thought, forcing a smile, certain that her lips must be blue. *I always get up in the middle of the night.*

"I came to start the fire in your stove." Ana stepped in and closed the door behind her. "These small cabins warm up fast. It will only take me a minute then you can get dressed in comfort." She bustled into the room with an apron full of kindling. Her cheeks glowed and her hair was held at the nape of her neck with orange and yellow chrysanthemums.

Jess squinted. "What time is it?" Her fingers fumbled across the desk for her watch.

"A little after six."

Good grief! Barely daylight. "Does everyone here

get up this early?" Jesseree moved over to the pot-bellied stove and shoved her hands at the feeble flames.

Anasuya gave a stir to the lit papers with a poker then half-closed the cast iron door leaving room for the air to circulate. "Heavens no." She reached up and adjusted the damper on the stove pipe. "We're the first ones up. The kitchen is the first place work begins." She turned and raised her brows. "There now. It's set." She pointed to the crackling fire. "You can add a small log in a minute. There's one out on the porch. Just make sure to close the stove door tightly before you leave. It only stays open until the fire gets going then it's important to remember to close it." She slammed the door then turned the handle hard. "There. Now I have to run and make bread. You know where the kitchen is, don't you?"

Jesseree nodded.

"The water tap is just outside between our cabins. You can fill a pan and heat it on the stove if you like. I wash with cold water. I find it stimulating." Ana turned and left as noiselessly as she had entered.

Jesseree scowled at the door and shuddered as she pulled her robe tightly around her. Had coming here been a mistake? She'd always credited herself for being an early riser, but not like this. In the dark and the cold. She eyed the warm sleeping bag tempted to climb back in. She shook her head. No. She'd brave it.

She crossed to the door and peeked out. A stack of small logs lay near the doorstep. When she reached around to grab one without stepping out on the cold porch, the sound of a snapping twig caught her attention. Two young deer standing near the corner of the cabin picked at leaves on the bushes.

"Hi, you guys," she called excitedly.

The deer looked up, stared, and turned, making their way back into the forest. When they were out of sight, she sucked in a deep breath. If rising early meant she could see them again, it might all be worth it. Back inside, she reached for her down jacket hanging from a metal hook. She spotted an enamel bowl to fill with water.

As she crunched across the mat of dry twigs to the water spigot, a trail of smoke streamed from the chimney of Ana's cabin. Jesseree smiled at her thoughtfulness. Tomorrow, she'd get up and build her own fire. Back a few feet between the two cabins, stood a smaller wooden structure. Jesseree winced at the chiseled sign, *WOMEN*. Of course a mountain retreat would have outside facilities. And the showers? Face it. She'd have to get used to roughing it. She nodded to herself. Last night she'd made a firm decision to stay here at Ahimsa for a full two weeks.

✷✷✷

"They'll be coming in any minute now from meditation," Ana called from across the kitchen. "Can you check the bread, Jess. Is it cool enough to slice?"

Jesseree touched the top of the sweet smelling loaves on the breadboard. "I don't know," she said uncertainly. "They still feel warm."

Ana was at the big stove, hands full of potholders. She reached into the oven. "We're only slicing two loaves for breakfast. Just cut through one end and see."

Aware from their first meeting up at the office, Ana could see Jess looked exhausted, that's why she had chosen her to help in the kitchen. She felt Jess might be more at ease under the direction of another woman for a while. At least until she settled in. She liked this city girl. For a San Francisco model, life at Ahimsa must seem like visiting another planet. Two weeks. That's about all it would take before the quiet atmosphere would relieve her tension.

Jesseree held up the dish. "I sliced it but it's uneven."

Anna looked up. "That's fine. Now, could you please put it out on the tables in the dining room? And Jess, could you take the honey, too?"

Jesseree removed the canvas apron and slipped off her down jacket. "Do you have any coffee?"

Ana pointed to the cupboard. "Paul's the big coffee drinker. He's given up meat but not his coffee."

Jesseree reached for a mug. "You don't eat meat here?"

"No. But you won't miss it. I guarantee. I'll teach

you how to prepare gourmet vegetarian dishes that will make your mouth water. When your system gets used to tofu, you'll feel terrific."

Jesseree picked up the bread and honey and placed them on a tray. "Who's Paul?"

Ana bustled past while she wiped her hands on her apron. "He's the fellow in the wheel chair. He lives here—gardens, lectures—a fantastic man."

Jesseree looked back at Ana. "Are you coming?"

"You go on ahead. I'll be along in a minute."

Jesseree hesitated at the door.

Ana smiled. "Go on. No one speaks in the morning. They've just returned from meditation."

Jesseree pushed open the door with her back before she turned to the people seated at two long tables. Sebastian gave her a warm welcoming smile. She returned his smile, steadied the pewter tray, and went on in.

ℰᏅℰᏅ

Jesseree climbed the hill to Eagle's Point, kicking aside pebbles and twigs on the winding path leading to the plateau. Breakfast had certainly been a bomb and all because of that snob, Devon. Earlier, when she had finished serving, Ana whispered for her to sit anywhere to eat breakfast, and Jesseree had chosen the empty space between Sebastian and Devon, two people she had already met.

After Sebastian's warm welcome, a smile and a light hand placed on her shoulder, she had looked to Devon for some sort of acknowledgement, but he hadn't bothered to even turn his head when she sat down. Throughout the rest of breakfast, she waited for any sign of recognition, even tried coughing twice, but to no avail.

She flushed angrily. Well, he could sit on it. Who did he think he was? He had dropped her like a hot biscuit in Sebastian's office yesterday, now he'd ignored her at breakfast. Yesterday when she arrived here, Sebastian mentioned that Devon might be the best friend she'd have in this lifetime. Ha! Never happening. Impossible to be friends with someone who refused to look at you. And then this job she'd been given of bussing and waiting tables. Probably Devon's suggestion. She made a face. Uh-huh. Not for her. She lifted her chin. She was a professional, accustomed to being paid for her effort. Not ignored.

When she finally reached the high plateau below Eagle's Point, she gasped for air as she struggled over to an old oak tree. Folding her down jacket into a cushion, she sat down heavily. Ana had suggested that she climb up here because of Jesseree's mood when she'd returned to the kitchen for cleanup. Ana finally asked what was bothering her, but Jesseree wouldn't say. She made it clear, however, that her negative attitude had nothing to do with Ana or the work.

She sat Indian style now with her elbows on her

knees and stared out into space. Why did this man's reaction to her matter? Go figure. She shook her head and nibbled at her lip. Something about Devon she couldn't define gnawed at her. Maybe because Sarah thought so much of him, Jesseree figured he must be deep—and warm—and loving. She sighed deeply. But if he was truly all of those things, he sure wasn't displaying any of those characteristics around her.

She needed his attention right now, damn it, to discuss Sarah and Sausalito and parts of her life she left behind in San Francisco. For some unexplained reason, she felt an urgency to tell him of the incident in Downieville. But why? Perhaps to ask him to help her figure out what that horrible calamity had been all about.

She shuddered, as once more she vividly pictured the hanging scene of the young man.

She frowned and spoke out loud. "Why would I want Devon to know?" Her life and what happened to her here, or anywhere else, was strictly her business, not his. Confused, she picked up a twig and tossed it, before leaning her head and shoulders back against the old oak tree. She finally closed her eyes and, as the morning sun seeped into her body, the anger and disappointment she felt for Devon slipped away.

It seemed like ages before she moved from the tree trunk and stood. Slowly crossing to the edge of the wide plateau, she marveled at the glorious view of mountains and forest.

Below, the entire retreat was laid out in various blocks of color and activity.

The main house, old and weathered, must have stood there for years. White shingled, two-story with an old-fashioned farmhouse front porch, it could have been someone's dream house years ago. Two newer additions had been added on each end of the porch. One held Sebastian's office on the west, and the other on the east, the kitchen. Partially hidden by the big house stood a white geodesic dome. Ahimsa's place of worship. She hadn't been there yet but this evening she planned to wander over and see what was happening.

Closer to the mountain, paralleling the huge vegetable garden, a building under construction looked like it might eventually become a greenhouse. Behind and to the side of the unfinished structure stood a small goat shed. Two figures below carried buckets to the animals. She listened closely and picked up the faint sound of the goat's neck bells as they frolicked about on the grass.

Closer in, she spotted her cabin next to Ana's and counted six more cabins encircling the edge of the forest. She squinted to see small furls of smoke from four chimneys. One of those chimneys, hers.

Feeling much, much better about her stay here at the retreat, she let the incident this morning at breakfast go and stretched high to the autumn sun as it streamed through the empty branches, energizing her head and arms.

Higher on the steepest side of the hill, red and gold leaves shimmered brightly. She carefully climbed up on the rocks and broke off an armful of branches. These would give a nice touch of color to the dining room tables. She smiled. Ana would be pleased.

She grabbed her jacket and eagerly turned to go back down the path. A man headed up. Jesseree's eyes narrowed. Devon! She turned in panic, searching for another way down. Damn! Only one path. And narrow. Rather than pass him, she decided to wait until he reached the plateau, keep her distance, then politely excuse herself, pass him, and leave.

Her anger returned with a rush as she recalled his rudeness.

"Good morning," he said, catching his breath.

Jesseree nodded stiffly.

"I didn't expect to find you up here." He glanced at the leaves and frowned. "Where are you going with those?"

"Excuse me," she said coolly.

He stepped aside as she brushed past him.

"I hope you're not planning to take those to the ashram."

She swung around. "What is it with you exactly? Is this place off limits?" She clutched the branches then strode down the hill

"Jesseree," he called after her.

She turned and glared up at him.

"Drop them!" he commanded.

"I don't know what your problem is," she said loudly. "If it's your macho image, you're trying to sell—forget it. I'm not buying."

"Jesseree!"

"*What*?"

"You're carrying poison oak!"

Chapter 13

The next afternoon a flash of excitement crossed Sebastian's face when Devon entered his office. Sebastian held a letter from India addressed to Devon. He couldn't be certain, but he had a feeling that the letter held good news for his friend. For weeks, Devon had been awaiting a letter of acceptance from a temple in the Himalayas—an acceptance from the Tibetan Lama for the post as an interpreter of ancient scrolls recently found buried in a sacred chest deep in the caves of Ranakpur.

Devon, a scholar of Sanskrit, spoke the numerous dialects necessary for the enormous project of translating the venerable parchments. He also possessed the spiritual discipline that made him valuable in assisting the Eastern masters with their tremendous undertaking.

If, indeed, Devon's letter requesting admission to this highest order was approved, Devon's leaving would be a sad parting for Sebastian. Sebastian would experience boundless joy for his associate, but he also realized that the Buddhist monks' gain would be Ahimsa's enormous loss.

The community here would all support Devon, emotionally as well as financially, in any way they could after his untiring work for the peace project. He certainly deserved a dividend. And since everyone at the ashram knew he desired this appointment with all of his heart, the people who shared his life wanted this appointment for him too.

Sebastian had known Devon for many years. Devon had been one of his English students at Berkeley during the late sixties. Those days seemed like another lifetime, and yet the two of them were still striving for the same cause now as they did back then—World Peace.

Devon had become a vital part of Ahimsa. Of the original twelve men who founded and built the retreat, only four were left. Throughout the years, most of the others had gone their separate ways. A thread of contact remained between them all, but Devon had stayed on to become Sebastian's confidant.

Ah yes. He would miss the many evenings they had shared over the years exchanging views while they worked late into the night on their lectures and lessons.

But if this letter that he held proved to be the turning point in their relationship, then Sebastian would be ready.

Now as Devon approached, Sebastian extended his hand. "The letter has come." He struggled to hide his excitement. "It came in this morning's mail."

Devon searched Sebastian's face. "Sent from Ranakpur?"

Sebastian nodded.

Devon carefully tore off the end of the envelope sealed with wax and removed a single folded sheet of paper. He scanned the black script then reverently folded the letter and placed it in his shirt pocket. When he looked at Sebastian, his eyes darkened.

Sebastian sighed. "The opening's been filled?"

"No." Devon shook his head. "On the contrary. I have been accepted."

Devon's sad smile confused Sebastian. "Then what? I thought you'd be elated."

"It's a privilege to have been accepted." Devon spoke slowly. "And you, above everyone else know how I have yearned to return to the land of my birth and be involved with these new-found mysteries." He folded his arms. "But there's a problem. Until I have it solved, I'm not worthy of the post."

Not worthy? No one on the planet could be worthier. Devon devoted himself to any task or assignment that he undertook. He gave of himself mentally and spiritually, as well as physically. No. Sebastian couldn't accept that.

Unless…Perhaps a personal problem. But what could be so serious as to prevent him from fulfilling his life's dream?

They had worked together for twelve years and Sebastian had faith now that whatever was burdening Devon could be worked out. He wouldn't probe. He would respect his friend's privacy. Yes, he nodded to himself. When Devon mastered his inner struggle, which no doubt would be soon, a positive decision could be made.

Sebastian placed his hand on his friend's shoulder. "Can I be of help?"

Devon turned away. "Perhaps later."

"All right then." Sebastian returned to his desk. "What will be your reply to the brothers?"

"I will write them that I'm not ready yet."

Devon walked out into the sunlight and looked up as dark clouds poured in over the mountain tops. They raced across the sky, cutting off a corner of the sun that hung low in the west. A shadow fell on Ahimsa and he felt the gloomy gray encircle his heart. Crumpling the long awaited envelope in his hand, he wandered across the meadow.

Why hadn't he been able to confide in Sebastian? He found it difficult to open up to others but he should be able to tell Sebastian. He shook his head. No. This issue involved his parents—the other woman in his father's life—and, most important, his feelings about it all.

He couldn't forget the pain in his mother's eyes that

day she found out about his father's infidelity. Though his father had been unfaithful to the family, Devon knew he must forgive him. He didn't have to condone the deed, but for himself he must forgive.

First, he would have to change his perception of what happened back then. That would be the difficult part. Hopefully, after he succeeded, he would be free at last to face his father and embrace him. Until he attained this, he felt he didn't deserve the post granted him by the holy monks.

He cut across the grounds and glanced over at Jesseree's cabin on the far side. Poor woman. He hadn't seen her since that unfortunate incident on the plateau with the poison oak leaves. Earlier at breakfast, he'd asked Ana about her. Ana explained that Jesseree was handling the misery of her allergy stoically.

He did regret that scene on the hill. His only concern at the time had been for her. But in his attempt to warn her of her actions, once again he'd been misunderstood. He knew she viewed him as controlling and bossy, but he only came across that way due to the uneasiness he felt whenever she was near.

He patted the letter smooth and placed it back in his pocket. Ironic how all of the past surfaced to haunt him just at this time when he should be the most joyful. This acceptance could open up a new life for him. One he'd dreamed of for years. Not only would he see his mother again, but he would be working in the most holy of places—a Himalayan temple. If the letter had arrived earlier, last week perhaps before he met Jesseree, he'd be packing now to leave.

The door to Jesseree's cabin swung open and Mary, the community's herbalist came out, holding her bag of dry herbs in one hand and a basket filled with small bottles of tinctures in the other. She set her bag down and waved. "We're open for visitors in here. Your energy would be appreciated if you have the time."

Mary, a big-boned Southern woman with hair the color of goldenrod, was an important member of the community. She and her husband, John, a carpenter, had been at Ahimsa for nearly eight years. Most of the buildings around the retreat held some of John's talent. He built cabinets and bookshelves with loving perfection and his name was well known by pleased customers in the nearby towns of Grass Valley and Nevada City.

Both from Kentucky, Mary and John added greatly to the workings of Ahimsa. Mary had learned most of what she knew about herbal healing from her granny back home. When she had moved to San Francisco, she'd continued her studies under the tutelage of a Sioux Indian.

She tended a huge herb patch near the vegetable garden and collected wild herbs that grew abundantly around the foothills. After harvesting and drying the medicinal plants, she packaged them in small brown bags and sold her concoctions to natural food stores from Reno to Sacramento. A competent practitioner, she treated most ills and accidents that happened at the retreat.

As Devon walked slowly toward Jesseree's cabin, Mary waited patiently, holding the door open.

Devon gave Mary a hug. "Is our guest feeling better?"

"Go on in and see. At least the itching is under control. The aloe has helped a lot and the mugwort has soothed her nerves. I've left tons of tea in there. Will you see that she drinks some of it?" She straightened the small bottles in her basket before she lifted it from the porch. "I've given her huge doses of vitamin C to combat the poison. Right now she's resting."

He took a deep breath. "Perhaps I shouldn't disturb her."

Mary widened the door. "Nonsense. You won't."

Devon sat down on the step. "I'll go in soon. I want to sit here a while."

As Mary took off toward the house, he reread his letter.

❧❧❧

Inside, Jesseree had been having a pity party. Between the pounding in her head and the itchiness of her skin, her nerves were shattered. Mary had come over, smeared aloe vera gel on her swollen face and arms, made a special tea, and then kept a watch while Jesseree drank. Mary had cooed sympathetically how this could have happened to anyone "—just anyone," and left Jesseree feeling better, more positive about making it through another night.

But the more tea she drank, the more often she had to get up, go outside and push through the door marked *WOMEN*.

"A little exercise won't hurt you none," Mary had drawled when Jesseree complained. "You just keep drinking the tea, hear? Would you rather be scratching or peeing?" She promised when she left that she'd come back tomorrow and start treating her homeopathically. "Then," she'd added confidently, "it won't be long before all the swelling's gone."

Jesseree hoped what Mary said was true. She didn't particularly care for herb tea but if that was what it took, she'd drink it until she floated.

Mary was speaking to someone outside. A man? Maybe Paul coming to visit again. What a sweetheart, pouring out sympathy along with the tea as he sat back in his wheelchair and sipped his coffee. Amazing how he could be so compassionate about her minor complaints when he was confined to a wheelchair.

They'd shared a lovely afternoon, talking about happenings around the retreat. When she'd asked about the silver rosary that hung from the arm of his chair, he took it in his fingers. "You mean my mantra? I'm Catholic and that rosary is my mantra. I use it at meditation."

Jesseree shook her head. "Sorry. You lost me."

"Mantra means sacred words—chanting," he explained. "It's kind of like a phone call to God—collect. When I get filled with anxiety or I get nervous, I need to relax and know who I am. What my Source is. That's when I repeat the mantra." He held the cross in his palm. "The name Jesus can be a mantra. Mantra is a Hindu word but it applies to all religions. When you hear chanting, *om—nama—shivaya* in the early morning, you know the Eastern Followers are preparing for meditation. The Christians usually repeat Jesus, Jesus, but I say my Hail Mary's. Sebastian says mana means mind and tri means to cross over. He says it's working to cross over the tumultuous sea of the mind."

Jesseree studied Paul's boyish face as he talked. "It's obvious you've accomplished that crossover .You seem calm."

Paul threw his head back and laughed. "Now, maybe yes. But you should have seen me when I first came here." He looked down at the holy chain between his fingers, and his face sobered. "I'm certainly not there yet but I'm working on it. When you're feeling better, why don't you join us for evening meditation?"

"I might." Jesseree held out her hand. "May I hold your rosary?"

Paul leaned over and placed it in her palm.

"It's beautiful." She outlined the small Christ on the crucifix with her fingertip. "It looks ancient—is it?"

"Belonged to my great-grandmother. It comes from Ireland. I always keep it with me. Always have it when I go to the cathedral."

Jesseree looked puzzled.

Paul laughed. "I call it the cathedral. Devon and some of the others say it's the temple. Mary and John are Protestants. They refer to the dome as their chapel."

"And what about the Jews? Is anyone Jewish?"

"Manu and Kapula. The men who raise goats. They've taken Eastern names. They feel it adds to their spirituality. But you know, it doesn't matter what anyone tags that manmade building, it's what happens there that's important. When we're all in there together, we realize we are One. We're all working toward the same cause. Peace. We know the importance of meditation and we practice it together."

Jesseree nodded. "I wasn't raised in a structured reli-gion. Most of what I know my grandmother's friend, Sa-rah, taught me. She's a mystic."

Paul smiled and raised a brow. "Lucky for you. Then you must join us."

That visit with Paul happened yesterday. Now she was looking forward to seeing him again. Opening her overnight bag, she looked at her face in the mirror. Winc-ing at the sight of the swelling, she carefully brushed her hair back and clipped it with a gold hairpin. She turned at a light rap on the door.

Devon's tall frame filled the doorway. His back was

to the afternoon light and Jesseree could barely make out his features. He presented the same image she'd seen that first night at Sarah's. The surprise at seeing him instead of Paul must have shown on her face because Devon hesitated at the door. "Am I disturbing you?"

"Come in," she offered and not too cordially. What did he want? Had he come to gloat over her stupidity? If he said one word…

He moved to a chair beside her bed. "May I sit?"

She nodded and felt a flush rise to her already-burning face. She scratched nervously around her hair-line.

"I'm sorry about the leaves," he began. "I was abrupt with you on the plateau. I guess I was acting…" He paused and raised an eyebrow. "…macho?"

She had to laugh. So out of character for him to say macho. Devon smiled when she laughed and, when she looked at him, their eyes met in a kinship that had been well hidden until that moment.

Suddenly shy, she offered, "A cup of tea?"

He nodded and got up to turn on the hot plate.

"I can do it." She started to stand.

He held up his hand. "Please. Rest."

She watched as he prepared the cups and brewed the tea. How handsome he looked. Dark hair and skin. Light eyes.

Whenever she looked into those eyes she felt a magnetic force that made it hard for her to look away.

She touched her face lightly with swollen fingertips. "I look a mess, huh?"

Devon turned. He studied her blotchy skin. "Not bad. Your skin is red like a strawberry. It's all relative. If you were a strawberry, you'd be considered beautiful. Think of your outer self as a berry for a couple of days, hidden under the shade of a big green leaf while the world busies itself around you. Take advantage of this time to relax before another stage of development begins."

Strange analogy, but she kind of liked it. He was being charming for a change and that was refreshing. Although he did seem somewhat preoccupied.

"How did your day go?" she asked, politely.

He mumbled something and for a moment she thought she'd lost him. She quickly turned the conversation in another direction. "Have you heard from Sarah?"

He brought the tea over. "No. I usually don't hear unless I call to say I'll be in her area. That's when she sends me a letter outlining her schedule."

Jesseree envisioned her old friend. "Amazing, isn't she?"

He agreed. Jesseree studied him and wondered about the change in his attitude. This was the first time they'd been alone except for their encounter at Eagle's Point. The afternoon light faded and Jesseree lit a lavender candle on the desk next to her bed. Devon stirred in his chair then settled back to drink his tea. The room grew still. It was as if neither one felt the need to talk. As the shadows deepened, the candle's steady flame flickered.

The bells from the temple called out for evening meditation and Devon stirred again. Placing his cup on the table, he got up, bowed to her then silently left.

She watched him go and a small stab of loneliness pierced her heart. She sighed deeply as the flame from the candle blinked, faltered, then rose to full wick brightness. She leaned back on her pillow, her brain whirling with thoughts of this strange man who stirred her senses. Warmth coursed through her as she remembered his hands when he poured the tea. Strong, tapered. Surely the hands of an artist.

Someday he might help her mold her life into something worthwhile, peaceful like his. He could very well become her teacher, and after their visit today, she wished to be his student.

Maybe someday soon they could hold hands in friendship and she'd be able to thank him for the lessons learned here at Ahimsa. Maybe.

Mary's concoctions were taking affect and calmness fell over her. The evening hours passed quickly and the comfort of Devon's visit lingered far into the night until the great autumn moon, shining through the small panes of the skylight sealed her tired eyes with ribbons of silver.

Before long, she slipped into a sleep full of gentle dreams of multi-colored lights and of a man wearing a satin turban with a flashing amethyst stone.

Chapter 14

Maureen swept a strand of auburn hair back from her face as she rushed around the side of her desk with a handful of white cards. She eyed the splashy office, done in plastic and leather, crowded with slim models and their acres of hair. Every available seat in the office was filled. Even the arms of chairs held small-bottomed women in tight-fitting jeans, eager to leave for their shoots.

She'd worked hard all morning to get the day's assignments out before ten. Now as she handed out the orders, the room shook with excitement. Everyone talked at once.

Occasionally a high-pitched laugh jarred her nerves and she flinched. Crazy Mondays. The two favorite topics that triggered the hoopla? Men or cosmetics. Most of the time, both.

She was ready to relax for fifteen. The morning had been a maze of phone calls from impatient clients, and now, her desk, covered with reams of paper to be filed as soon as everyone left, caused her shoulders to sag.

Mr. Crandal, in a tailored pinstriped suit, had passed by her desk earlier and shot her a curt nod. He could have at least offered a smile. Given her a bit of encouragement for the busy day ahead. She scowled over at his door marked *Private*, and made a mental note to see him later about hiring someone part-time to help out.

After the cards were handed out, a few models headed for the elevator, stuffing appointment schedules into their oversized bags. She counted the remaining heads still waiting for a conference with Mr. Crandal, and tapped her chin with her finger. Too many. She'd just have to take them alphabetically and hope for the best. Brushing at the stray lock of her hair, she licked her parched lips then turned to the water cooler across the room. Her eyes widened in surprise at the sight of a man leaning against the wall next to Mr. Crandal's door. The guy's face was the color of cement and his scarlet-rimmed eyes stared at her unblinkingly. When had he come in?

She moved closer then hesitated. "Jacob? Jacob Kelso?" The stench of alcohol and stale smoke nearly sent her off balance. He looked awful—wrinkled clothes, dirty fingernails, stringy hair touching the collar of his once-white shirt.

"Where's Jess?" he demanded in a hoarse voice.

Maureen panicked. Something about the way he said Jess. Weird vibrations pricked at her skin and she knew she'd have to use tact to prevent a scene. This guy wasn't going to settle for any I-don't-know routines.

"Look, Jacob," she whispered. "I've got a break coming up soon. Why don't we talk about Jess over coffee?"

His hand shot out and grabbed her arm, pulling her close. Behind the stench of booze, the rankness of his dirty clothes made her nauseous. A sudden fear churned her stomach. Jess's words, '*He's been acting strange,*' pounded across her mind. She looked up and Jacob's eyes flared with rage.

She glanced over her shoulder. The models, still caught up in their own conversations, were unaware of anything amiss. Silently vowing not to call out unless absolutely necessary, she looked back at Jacob "Let go." She winced. "You're hurting me."

"Where is she? I'm not waiting for any coffee break."

Maureen struggled to twist out of his grip. "I don't know where she is." The blood drained from her head and she felt dizzy. The green door behind Jacob blurred. "Jacob. Let me go. I'm going to faint." Her knees buckled and two concerned models jumped up. Jacob grabbed her around the waist. With a menacing glare at the women, he reached back and shoved open the door marked *Private*. He pulled Maureen into the office with him and kicked the door shut.

Crandal sprang from his desk chair. "What the hell?" He reached under his desk and pressed the emergency button. "Maureen," he demanded. "What's going on? Who is this?"

Jacob held her tight and by now she was too weak to struggle. He gasped for breath and she could feel his tense body tremble. His heart pounded wildly against her back. She groaned when he suddenly shifted his grasp to include her wrist.

"Shut up," Jacob shouted at Crandal. "I want to know about one of your models. Right now." He glanced down at Maureen. The terror she felt shone in her eyes and he relaxed his grip. She slumped to the floor, supporting herself on the arm of the leather sofa. With careful effort she crawled up on the cushion and sat very still.

For a moment Jacob scanned the private office, seemingly aware of his surroundings. He turned to Maureen. "I don't want to hurt anybody."

His unexpected change of tone gave Crandal an edge. He quickly moved around the side of his desk toward Maureen on the sofa. "Who are you," he demanded. "What do you want with Maureen?"

Jacob pointed a shaky finger at Crandal, stopping him in his tracks. "Just tell me where Jess is."

So that was it! Damn models and their love lives. Crandal glared at the intruder standing across from him and wondered if he had a weapon concealed in his wrinkled jacket. Tempted to rush Jacob and hold him until the security guard arrived, he changed his mind. With crackpots like this you never knew what to expect. He could be armed. Crandal glanced impatiently at the door. Where the hell was that guard?

Maureen rubbed her arm. "Jacob," she pleaded. "Relax. Sober up."

"Don't tell me what to do," he snapped. "I want Jess and I'm going to find her." He shot a defiant look at Maureen then glared over at Crandal.

For a moment the room was deathly still then Maureen could hear the buzz of excited models on the other side of the door. She looked up at Mr. Crandal and he gave her a confident wink. Jacob moved to the sofa and dropped down next to Maureen. He leaned his head back. "Just tell me where she is," he pleaded. His red eyes were moist and his voice shook. "I can't leave until I find her."

Maureen's fear turned to compassion. "She'll be back." She rubbed her arm. "That's all I know. Really, Jacob."

The door burst open and the security guard rushed in while a dozen pretty heads peered over his shoulder. Crandal pointed at Jacob and growled, "Grab him! "The guard jerked Jacob up by his shirtfront and frisked him.

"Okay, jerk. Let's move it on out of here." He looked to Crandal for instructions. "Should I have him picked up?"

This wasn't the first romantic outburst Crandal had seen in twenty-two years at Kurlay. But it was the most frightening. And right here in his private office. A man wasn't safe anyplace with all these crazies running loose. He studied Jacob. Now that things had simmered down, he recognized him as Jesseree's friend. He'd seen him a few times in the outer office. But never in this condition.

Poor bastard! Beautiful models will drive a man crazy every time.

Maureen held her breath. She felt torn now in her feelings for Jacob. What would Mr. Crandal decide to do? Jacob had looked so small and thin crumpled beside her on the sofa. There was no denying he could be dangerous. For sure, he needed help.

Crandal cleared his throat. "Don't ever enter this agency again. If you do, I'll have you arrested." He went back to his desk and scribbled a memo. "I'm having a restraining order put on you."

Jacob's chin hung to his chest. A thin line of water escaped from one nostril and clung to his upper lip. Dark unclipped curls tumbled around his ears and when he looked up, a childlike expression haunted his face.

Crandal motioned to the guard. "Get him out of here."

Maureen trailed behind as the guard held Jacob and pressed their way through the curious onlookers. Back at her desk, she opened a drawer and removed her purse. She rummaged through until she found a card with Sarah's number.

Chapter 15

Dear Jess,
Don't get excited. I'm not trying to get into your space. I know you wanted to get away from all the stress here in the city but I thought I should write and tell you what's been happening. I called your friend, Sarah, and she gave me your address.

You're right about Jacob, sweetie. He hasn't got both oars in the water. He was here at the agency yesterday, rabble rousing, and the last I saw of him, he was being escorted to the elevator by the security guard while a group of models cheered him on.

Honestly! Some of them are really weird!

Jacob doesn't know where you are. No one knows, except me and Sarah. So you're safe to finish your vacation in peace. I pumped Sarah for information about where you are and I think it's great. Is there a chance I could come up there and visit—maybe a weekend retreat before you come back? I know it's your thing and if you don't want to see anyone from the city, I understand. I miss you, Jess. There's no one around here to talk to. I mean really talk to. If I don't hear from you, have a nice Thanksgiving. Do they celebrate it up there?

Anyway—Love ya, Maureen.

PS, When I talked to Sarah, she said to tell you she'll be in the foothills soon visiting friends in nearby Grass Valley.

Jesseree let the typed letter fall into her lap while she gazed out over the valley. Once again, she sat under the old oak on the plateau, a spot that had become her favorite sorting-out place. She wondered if Maureen could possibly be making light of this incident with Jacob.

She'd hoped by now that he was getting his life together and buckling down in school. Though she really hadn't given him much thought lately, this letter started the wheels rolling as she faced the prospect of going home.

Straightening her spine against the trunk of the old

tree, she leaned her head back and closed her eyes. She wished Jacob would get on with his life and forget about her. The way she felt now, she didn't care to ever see him again.

And Maureen. Jesseree felt guilty for involving her friend in this mess, but then who could have predicted that Jacob would go to her agency? She glanced at the letter. Rabble rousing. That could mean anything. If he didn't stop acting out and going to her agency, he could cause her to lose her job.

The morning sun warmed her face as she tried to center her thoughts on positive aspects of their past relationship. She really wanted a peaceful closure with Jacob, but at this point that didn't seem probable. Daily she'd been working on incorporating into her life the principles outlined by Sebastian and Devon when they spoke about peace at group meetings. Already, she'd made friends here with good people who cared about each other. They treated each other with respect. She'd observed combined energies directed toward bettering the planet. Each day she learned new theories from these dedicated people. But applying them emotionally had become extremely difficult for her.

"Don't worry, Jess," Sebastian told her yesterday. "It took the Buddha seven years to reach Samadhi, union with the Lord. Don't rush it. Your time will come. You've been here less than three weeks."

He was right of course. But patience was not her

strong point. Soon, she'd have to return to her job and she needed Olympic courage and stamina to face what she'd left behind.

Jess smiled to herself, recalling Ana's remark when Jess joined her in the kitchen after morning meditation. "I can't believe it. You look like a new person. Your cheeks are pink, eyes are clear, and at last you're not so cold. No more bundling up."

Yes. She'd gained weight and was sleeping sounder. No more sinking nightmares. Eating Ana's nourishing breakfasts and breathing the clear mountain air had done wonders for her. But most important, her friendship with Devon had blossomed. She found him brilliant as well as handsome. His teaching methods were simplified so that a layperson like herself could sit in on an ongoing class and pick up the thread of his philosophy without too much trouble.

She smiled. And lately, he seemed to be seeking her out. Whenever they were in the same room, she could feel his gaze. He no longer turned away when their eyes met. Sometimes when they were together, they stood lost in each other's light until it was embarrassingly obvious to the others around them.

Later today when her chores in the kitchen were done, and Devon's notes for his next peace lecture were completed, they planned to go down the hill to his favorite spot near the creek that ran into the Yuba River. He called it Bhakti, his place of Divine Services. "It's a sandy beach," he'd explained earlier. "A place I would like to share with you."

Delighted to be included in something so personal, she daydreamed of sitting alone with him next to the water. A rushing sensation filled her senses, and she wished he were here now, sitting on this mountain beside her under the tree.

She heard a shuffling noise in front of her and she opened her eyes, expecting to see a small animal scurrying through the leaves. Not an animal, but a man in a white robe, carrying a carved staff, climbed the winding path to the plateau. His sandaled feet were dusty and his shaved head glistened in the morning sun.

She shifted to get up then decided to stay put. When he reached the plateau, he stopped and shook the hem of his robe, releasing a small cloud of red dust and leaves. Taking a deep breath, he looked all around, observing the hills and valleys. The air stilled and the sun brightened as the robed man planted his staff firmly on the ground in front of him, placing one hand over the other. A low rumbling rose from deep inside of him, shaking the ground as it turned into a chant echoing out across the valley. Startled at first, Jesseree remained seated beneath the tree but in seconds she felt a sudden warmth flow through her, bringing a peace she'd never experienced before. The mighty power of the chant brought her to her feet and she stood tall under the bare branches of the old oak.

The robed man turned to face her and a brilliant white light formed around him. She stood transfixed staring into the depths of his radiant eyes. Time and the world stood still while she bathed in the glorious light that now surrounded them both.

After what seemed like forever, the white-robed man turned. She watched with regret as he proceeded effortlessly upward on the sheer face of the cliff until he reached Eagle's Point and quietly disappeared over the crest.

"It's not surprising to me that you met this monk up there," Devon said when she told him her experience. "Here at Ahimsa you're treading on hallowed ground. In the early fifteen hundreds, white-robed Dominican Friars had their sanctuary here. They were men of great spirit who devoted their lives to defending the Indians. They settled here when they fled to escape persecution from their Spanish brothers."

He placed a blanket on the sand and motioned for Jesseree to sit. "Then much later," he continued, "during the late-eighteen hundreds, Chinese monks strolled these hills during the gold rush." He studied her. "It's a possibility you had an esoteric vision."

Jesseree looked puzzled. "You're saying he wasn't real? That's hard to believe."

"Hold on. It's obvious to me you have vision far greater than most. I believe that in this situation time was irrelevant. There could be an indelible monastery above

Ahimsa, carrying on day-to-day life, the same as us. We don't see each other because we're living in different dimensions. Unless, of course, someone like you with an exceptional gift comes along. Then all barriers are broken."

She leaned back on her elbows. That might be true. But she had really hoped that the monk was real. Flesh and blood because she longed to be in his presence again. The experience this morning differed greatly from the horrifying vision in Downieville. When she had finally confided to Devon her experience there, he'd been most sympathetic.

He sat next to her now, thoughtfully drawing symbols in the sand with a pointed stick. "Does my theory make any sense to you?"

Jesseree nodded. "A little. I know that if Sarah were here, she would probably agree with you."

Devon laughed. "It's her influence that directs me. She's certainly one who knows."

"Have you known her a long time?"

"Years. I met her when I lived in Berkeley. Actually Sarah was Sebastian's friend. She taught modern dance at the university. Sebastian taught there too. One night a group of us went to her home for a *satsang*, a spiritual fellowship, and we three have been in contact ever since.

"Why did I think you've known her since you were a child?"

Devon shrugged. "I have no idea."

They watched in silence as the water rushed toward the big river. Finally Jesseree spoke. "Did you read history books about the Dominicans and the Chinese monks?"

"Not really. Sarah informed us of the history when she gave us this land. She'd done a lot of research corroborating the spiritual energy that surrounds this property."

"Ahimsa belonged to Sarah?"

"You didn't know?"

Jesseree shook her head. "She didn't mention any of this when she suggested I come here."

"It belonged to her and David, her husband killed in World War Two. They invested in this property with the idea of using the white house as their summer home when he returned from the Pacific. But as you know…Twenty years later, Sebastian and I assumed the mortgage.

So that was Sarah's dream house. Figured. Her style. Two stories with a farmhouse porch. "Does she come here often?"

"Not often but she's coming for the Indian Feast the first of November. She never misses the celebration. Do you know about it?"

Jesseree nodded. "Ana and I are already baking dishes for the event."

"Good." He smiled. "Then that means you're planning to stay." He touched her arm affectionately. "You and Sarah will be here together."

Jesseree moved closer to the stream. "Getting back to

the monk. Do you think I'll ever see him again?"

"Do you want to?"

"Yes, very much."

"Then there's a strong possibility you will."

"I don't ever want to see anything like Downieville again." She shivered. "I haven't figured out what that was all about."

Devon stared out across the stream to a boulder where a squirrel chewed an acorn. "It still disturbs you, doesn't it?"

"Sure. I don't know what it meant." She reached into the clear water for a pebble. "If what you believe is true, that we sometimes relive the same situation over and over with the same people until we get it right, then I have a reason to be upset."

"Nothing's written in stone," he said. "When we reach a point in our evolution and say enough, I want an end to all of the nonsense that causes me sorrow, then the order shifts. When our consciousness changes, our life must change accordingly."

Her lower lip trembled. "Somehow," she said, avoiding his eyes. "I felt you were part of that awful scene in Downieville. I'm not sure how. I feel certain the young girl with the scarf was me. I felt like I stood above her body—my body—watching them revive her."

Her eyes filled with tears. "Death surrounded me that day." She folded her arms tightly. "I shudder when I think about it. This morning on the plateau, that may have been a gift, but Downieville—that had to be a retribution.

Devon's voice lowered. "You don't involve me in your visions, Jesseree. If I was there, it's because of my own actions." He moved closer to her and she could feel his warmth. "Remember that we are masters of our destinies. There is nothing that can't be changed."

The afternoon sun disappeared behind the trees and a chilly breeze blew up from the water. They both jumped up, grabbing the blanket and their jackets. Devon guided a worried Jesseree back to the ashram.

Chapter 16

Anasuya carefully packed the last carob cookie into the white pastry box and tied it with string. After a long morning of baking, the kitchen looked like a disaster had hit. While Jesseree hurriedly straightened up, Ana sorted the baked goods into groups of cookies, fruit breads, and rolls as she prepared to go on the monthly trip to Nevada City where the store merchants purchased their goods.

Earlier, the retreat's van had been loaded with ice chests full of goats' milk, yogurt, and cheese made by Kapul and Manu.

Mary's Miracles, herbs brightly packaged and neatly marked, were crowded near the front of the van to make room for Ana's baked goods plus two handcrafted oak bookcases John had stayed up late to finish.

"I'm so glad you're coming along today, Jess." Ana smiled. "It's time you got out. It will be fun to shop and have lunch." She glanced around the kitchen "Just let the dishes go. Two visiting students from Gold Dust offered to clean up so we can get an early start." She made a tight bow of the string. "Devon's coming, isn't he?"

Jesseree nodded. She had been helping him for three days, typing and doing paste-ups for pamphlets to be dropped off at the printers. Now when he left to lecture again, his research material advocating a nuclear freeze would be completed and ready for distribution.

Ana picked up two boxes. "You know," she said thoughtfully. "It's really a shame Devon is turning down that position in the Himalayas. We were all planning to have his going away party combined with the Indian Feast. But now." She sighed. "I guess we'll just have to wait."

Jesseree paled. "Devon's leaving Ahimsa?"

Ana turned at the shock in Jesseree's voice. "He planned to go," she said carefully. "He's been accepted. I hope he changes his mind." She hesitated before continuing. "Working in that temple has been his dream."

Jesseree quickly turned away.

"What is it, Jess? Didn't he tell you?"

Jesseree fought for control. "No. He hasn't said anything to me about leaving."

Ana crossed to where Jesseree stood staring out the

window. "I've upset you. I thought everyone here knew."

"It's all right, Ana. I'm glad you told me. Really I am. I'm surprised, that's all." She gripped the edge of the sink. "When did you say he's leaving?"

"I didn't. He's decided to wait. There's some personal problem he's working on."

Rain clouds swept in over the hills and Jesseree watched as they merged. "Well, if we're going, we'd better leave soon. A storm is on its way."

Ana carefully closed and taped a pastry box. "I won't be through for a while, Jess. If you have something else to do, I can handle things here."

Jesseree nodded. "If you're sure you can manage, I'll run over and see if Devon needs help sorting papers."

She rapped on the cabin door. It opened and Devon's head appeared. The door widened and Jesseree stepped in. "I hoped you'd come." He clipped typed pages together and placed them in his briefcase. "I wanted to thank you again. Because of your help, the information for the brochures is ready to go, and I've met the printer's deadline." He glanced out the window at the van. "Are they leaving?"

"Not yet." Jesseree grabbed a handful of paper clips and joined him. Her hands felt as cold as her heart. "Devon?"

He turned and raised his eyebrows.

"Do you trust me?"

"That's a strange question."

"Well, do you?"

"Haven't I entrusted you with all of my scribblings?"

"That's not what I mean."

"Jesseree?" Devon looked concerned. "What is it?"

She glanced down at her hands. "The Himalayas. I just found out." Her voice shook. "Apparently, you don't trust me enough to tell me you're leaving."

"Jesseree," His voice took on a gentle tone. "Sit down."

"We don't have time." She shrugged. "The van's almost packed. Everyone will be waiting for us."

"We do have time." He searched her face. "You're hurt."

"Ridiculous." She dropped to the chair. "I'm not hurt. Just disappointed. It's dishonest to keep quiet about something as important as this. Didn't you think I'd be interested, or what?"

He sat down across from her. "You feel left out."

"Of course I do. And I'm confused. Wouldn't you be?" She straightened. "No. Maybe you wouldn't. You're too damn independent." She looked past him to the far wall lined with his books. "When two people are friends, they share important decisions."

"They do," he agreed. "And you are my friend. I would tell you if I had made that decision. But I haven't," he added sadly, "Perhaps I never will."

She jumped up and crossed to the door. "I guess it really doesn't matter. I'll be leaving soon myself to go back to the city." The wind started up and she could see Ana across the meadow, her skirt whipping about her ankles as she ran from the van back to the kitchen to collect more boxes. "If or when you decide to go, are you leaving for good?"

Within seconds he reached her. "I've been a fool. I should have told you about the temple. Instead, I let you hear it from someone else."

Jesseree shook her head hopelessly. "Didn't you think I'd care?"

"I know you care." He hesitated. "I also knew if I started to explain, I'd tell you everything. And most of it's painful for me."

Jesseree turned and gazed up into his eyes. "Devon. It's important to me that I know."

They stood in the open doorway until Devon turned and led her back inside. As the wind gained momentum and the dark clouds swirled above, the two returned to their chairs. With great difficulty, he told her the story of his parent's breakup.

He dug deep into the past probing the wound that, until recently, he had convinced himself was healed. Healed until that fateful night at Sarah's. He spoke of his mother's unhappiness and of his father's apparent insensitivity to her needs. Finally, he haltingly revealed his father's affair with the American woman, and of the letter that had sent his mother fleeing back to her native India.

"I suppose I've never worked myself free of my

mother's pain," he added thoughtfully. "And I've felt guilty for refusing to return to India with her. I fooled myself into believing that I had forgiven my father for all of her unhappiness, but I realize that's not true. All of these years I've avoided him, convincing myself I'm too busy. That we had nothing in common. He would never understand my work here. I salved my conscience with lies—until I met you.

"That night at Sarah's, you were so beautiful that, for an instant, I identified with my father. I wondered if the attraction I had for you matched the powerful attraction he'd felt for his American woman. The woman completely different from my mother. When Sarah asked for my help in healing your swollen ankle, it took all the energy I could summon to kneel by your side." His voice broke. "For some unexplained reason you represented that unknown woman. A woman I resented."

The wind ripped at the shutters of the cabin. A scraping noise outside on the porch caused Devon to turn. Jesseree didn't budge. Her eyes never left his face.

"I only agreed to let you come to Ahimsa," he continued, "because Sarah asked. Since you've been here, our friendship has grown and now I see your true inner beauty." He waited for Jesseree to respond but she sat perfectly still. "Until I get all of these feelings sorted out regarding my father and his American woman, my work in India will have to wait." He sighed deeply. "That's it, Jesseree. The whole story." He stood and crossed to an old brown trunk in the corner. He rummaged through and brought out the blue letter his mother had found all those years ago and placed it on the table between them. "You may read it if you like."

Jesseree pushed the paper away. "No. Thank you." As it slid across the table it unfolded revealing a bold inked signature, Star, at the bottom of the page. "I really don't care to read your father's private mail. And I'm surprised you did. Why do you have it, anyway? Especially after all this time."

He shrugged and placed it back in the trunk. "I really didn't read it again until recently. And I don't know why I still have it. The day my mother left for India, she threw it in the trash. I pulled it out with the intention of confronting my father with it and demanding to know who this woman was. But I didn't. I didn't realize then that there is no peace without conflict."

"Why did you have to know this woman?"

"I wanted to see her." He shrugged. "Curiosity, I suppose."

Jesseree could hardly believe this—Devon giving up a dream for something that had happened fifteen years ago. Something that didn't involve him anymore. "You were grown when all of this happened, Devon. I don't understand what your problem is."

"I've never forgiven my father. Can't you see how I felt?" He reached out and touched her sleeve. "I've tried to understand your problems. Your relationship with Jacob—your grandmother's bitterness. The pressures of your job."

She inched her arm away. "I believe I can understand how you felt then. But that scene happened between your father and mother. Can't you see that now?" Her voice had an edge as she fought to save her guru as he crumbled around his clay feet. "I'm having a problem believing you haven't resolved all of this." She made a wide sweep with her arms. "Everything you teach here—your entire philosophy is love. You tell your students to let go of the past and you can't. What kind of a teacher are you?"

She stood up, hands folded in front of her. "Look past the *samskaras*, you tell us. Past the obsessive personality traits of your brothers and sisters. Look for the golden seed of love planted deep within their hearts. You teach this, Devon, and I've memorized it. 'Peace begins in the home,'" she recited. "'There will be no world peace until we find it there first.' You tell us all this and you can't forgive your father and this—this—" Her voice grew shrill. "—this other woman."

She dropped back to her chair and her voice softened. "I don't want you to go away, Devon. You're probably the best friend I've ever had." She spoke with her head bowed. "But if the temple work is what you really want, then I want it for you, too. You'll never really know what went on between your parents. Or your father and the other woman."

A flash of insight regarding her own childhood stopped her. For years her grandmother's bitterness against her father had been affecting her life. Until this moment, she hadn't been able to see her own problem clearly. She had never forgiven her father for drinking on the night of the boating accident. For years, she had been sitting in judgment of not only her father, but all men.

Devon reached over and covered her hand with his. She smiled sadly. She should be comforting him, instead of lecturing. At this moment, she longed to hold him, re-assure him but she held back. When he sorted this all out and it came time for him to leave, their goodbye would be hard enough.

He looked at her steadily. "Please, Jesseree. Don't think badly of me. I've been working hard to solve this problem. But you know." His eyes narrowed thoughtful-ly, "I think something you said might be the key." He glanced over at the trunk. "That letter has been eating away at me all these years. Shadowing my life." He crossed to the trunk, removed the letter, and held it up like some negative banner. Striking a match, he set fire to the blue edge and placed it in an incense tray on the table.

They both watched as the orange flame wrinkled the paper, turning it into black smoke. When all that re-mained were the ashes, Devon brushed his hands off. "There. The second step of healing has taken place. The first? Learning who you truly are. Now I'll work at find-ing out who my father really is. Maybe then the years of pain will disappear like the words on that letter."

A knock on the door and Ana peeked in. "We're ready to leave."

Devon and Jesseree gathered up the remaining papers from the desk and placed them in his briefcase. The three ran against the wind across the meadow to the waiting van.

Chapter 17

On the way back from the outing, the van bumped over the dirt road leading to the ashram entrance. Devon and Jesseree sat side by side on the van's worn leather seat, her hip pressed firmly against his as the van swayed and made sharp turns on the mountain curves. Devon had the window seat, and since they'd left town, he'd grown quiet. Earlier at his cabin, he had shared the sorrow of his past. Perhaps now, he regretted confiding in her.

He'd seemed in good spirits on the trip down to Nevada City, and optimistically joined in with the others as they looked forward to selling their products in town. When early plans for the Indian Feast were discussed, he made valuable suggestions on setting up booths and tents.

And he'd laughed heartily when John told them how one of the retreat goats tried to eat his paintbrush, and how John raced after the bell-ringing goat, pulled the brush from his mouth, causing both John and the goat to be splattered with green paint.

But now on the slow climb home, Devon seemed depressed, and Jesseree regretted that she had been so sharp with him this morning over his parent's breakup. If that's what bothered him now, when the time was right, she would explain her reaction. Explain how she looked to him for guidance and if he still grappled with family problems from the past, what chance did she have to work out her resentments before she had to leave Ahimsa? At least he had confided in her. Next time she would try to be more sympathetic, not judgmental, and when they returned to Ahimsa, she planned to go to his cabin and tell him so.

She leaned back against the seat. Nevada City had been fun. When they arrived, the group had split up. Devon was dropped off at the printers, papers in hand. The Dairy Boys, as Sebastian affectionately referred to them, along with Ana and Mary, had all been let out at the Carrot Top Natural Food Store. Jesseree asked for a boutique, and John stopped and opened the van door in front of The Singing Crystal, a shop with a window filled with lights. Before he drove off to deliver his furniture, they agreed to meet the rest of the group at The Carrot Top Food Bar for lunch at one-thirty.

Jesseree made it there on time, but by two fifteen, Devon hadn't shown. She picked at her salad while she kept her eye on the entrance to the store. When the others finished eating, they decided to go outside and look for him.

No sign of him, but Ana spotted a note from Devon slipped under the windshield wiper asking to be picked up at the bookstore.

"Why didn't you join us?" Mary said as he climbed into the back seat.

"Not hungry," he mumbled.

He pressed against the window with his briefcase balanced on his knees. Jesseree sat next to him eager to show him the filigree earrings she'd purchased for the Indian Feast. But the wall of silence he'd built between them cautioned her to wait.

When they arrived at Ahimsa, everyone helped unload the van. Jesseree turned to ask Devon if he needed help with typing, but he was gone, striding across the meadow headed for the main house. As he neared the greenhouse, Paul rolled his chair quickly down the path calling his name. Devon stopped and waited until he caught up. She watched as the two men exchanged greetings before she reached into the van for her purse and package. When she turned back, they were both out of sight.

එනෙන

Jesseree slipped off her shoes and entered the temple for evening meditation. On a carpeted platform, near the wide paneled windows that overlooked the trees, Sebastian sat in an antique padded chair, his arms resting easily by his sides, palms turned upward on his lap.

Anasuya, dressed in three shades of purple, sat on the platform near his feet accompanying herself on a harmonium while she softly sang a melodic chant. With her eyes closed and legs crossed in dedication, she bent over the teakwood instrument, pumping the bellows with one hand while she deftly ran her fingers over the keys with the other.

The tilt of her head allowed her dark hair, plaited and entwined with lavender ribbon, to rest on her shoulder as her bell-like voice led the residents and students of the ashram in the preliminary music for meditation.

Jesseree joined in the singing, humming along, not knowing the words, while she studied the people around her. A beauty seemed to flow from their calm faces as they prepared themselves for their inner journey. She spotted Devon down in front near the platform and watched him as he sang. She strained to hear his voice but she couldn't distinguish his sound from the others that filled the dome.

She wondered if he was thinking of his parents as he sang. Now that she'd gained some understanding of his problem, she vowed to be more compassionate if he spoke of his family again.

Next time if it happened, she would try to be more supportive.

As she watched and listened, a solid yellow light formed around Devon. She blinked and the light grew brighter. Recalling Sarah's explanation of auras being energy fields, she was delighted to have this opportunity to see Devon bathed in his own inner power.

She began to squirm impatiently, desiring to share this important moment with him, but she had no choice except to wait. Long after the music stopped and the temple grew quiet, she sat unmoving, staring, longing to enter his aura but feeling bound to the spot where she sat.

Eventually her eyes closed, but even then she could still see the yellow light. Before long, a presence flooded her being. With a sudden quickening of energy, she found herself traveling through a tunnel filled with the same light that encircled Devon. She flew along the lighted tunnel until she reached the end and settled near the bank of a quiet pool filled with lotus flowers.

Aware of a figure in a white robe standing beside her, she looked up. The monk from the plateau gazed deeply into her eyes. A multi-colored butterfly passed between them and landed on her shoulder. She turned her head to see. When she looked back, the monk had gone.

Sebastian's voice broke through the stillness with the benediction, "Om—Shanti—Shanti—Shanti."

Jesseree opened her eyes. The group remained seated for a few moments longer. Soon, one by one, they filed out of the dome. Paul, who had been seated near the wall during meditation, rolled his chair next to her and affectionately touched her shoulder before moving on.

Sebastian and Mary smiled as they passed her on their way out. She returned their smile and waited for Devon. When he didn't move from his meditative posture, she stood and stretched before she slipped on her shoes and left.

After dinner, back in her cabin, Jesseree opened the squeaky metal door and peered into the stove. No hot coals beneath the grate. She shut the door and shivered. Buttoning her down coat and pulling it tight across her chest, she ventured outside with her flashlight. First she dropped dried pinecones into an enamel bucket on the porch. Next, she filled her arms with kindling and grabbed a small log from a stack next to the door. Back inside, she set everything on the braided rug.

Pleased with herself, she nodded. Since she'd been here she had become a pretty fair fire builder. At first, she would kneel down and blow air into the opening trying to get the sticks to ignite, but now she knew exactly how much paper and wood to stuff in the belly of the stove before she lit that first match.

When the fire blazed, she carefully shut the door and pulled the handle down tightly as Ana had instructed. Wrapping her jacket closely around her, she pulled the bamboo chair over near the heat. Warming her feet, she wondered about Devon. After meditation, he didn't show up for dinner. When she had asked Ana about him, she'd said she hadn't seen him since meditation.

Somehow Jesseree didn't feel comfortable going to sleep tonight without talking to him, explaining about their earlier conversation regarding his parents. She could go to his cabin on the pretense of borrowing a book but he would see through her. No. She would go over and knock and...and what? If he was trying to work through his problem, he might resent her intrusion. Sometimes after people revealed too much of themselves, they craved privacy. She knew she did. Come on, she told herself, stop psyching him out. If she wanted to get any rest tonight, she better go on over.

Wet grass brushed her ankles as she trudged across the meadow. She pulled her wool scarf around her mouth and nose, filtering out the cold air. The evening cloud cover had now disappeared and silver stars blinked through the moonless sky. A dim light in Devon's cabin beckoned her on.

When she reached his door, a sudden warning gripped her stomach. She stopped and stood alone in the dark, trying to decide whether to go or stay. Before she could make a decision, Devon's cabin door opened and he stepped out.

"Hey," she called uncertainly. "Were you just leaving?"

He searched through the darkness. "I thought I heard someone knock."

"You almost did." Her step quickened. "Were you ready to go to sleep?"

"No." His tone was distant. "Reading." When she reached him they stood there in the cold facing each other.

Jesseree shivered. "Aren't you going to ask me in?"

He stepped aside for her to pass. "Of course."

For a fraction of a second, she stood in his doorway struggling with that warning feeling again, but being near him like this, she ignored the danger signals. When she stepped in, Devon closed the door behind them.

Before many minutes, the warning signals she'd been given materialized when Devon handed her a magazine he'd picked up at a bookstore in Nevada City.

"So what are you suggesting—I quit my job?" Her voice rose as she flipped through the pages of the magazine. "You forget that's how I make my living."

"I know that," he said. "But can't you be more selective about what you advertise?" He pulled another magazine from his briefcase. "How can you sell alcohol when you've told me how you feel about drugs?"

She glanced at her watch with impatience. They had been arguing about her pictures in the magazines for over forty-five minutes, and she'd thought he was keeping his distance because she wasn't sympathetic about his family problem. If she hadn't made it a point to come over here tonight, who knows when he'd have told her what really bothered him?

"I have to work, Devon. I'm not rich. Sure. I don't always get the shoots I desire but the competition is fierce out there. I need the money. It's expensive to live in San Francisco."

He shook his head. "You don't have to do anything. You told me you were one of the highest paid models in the Bay Area."

"Yes. And that's why. Because I accept what I'm offered. If I didn't take these jobs, there's at least fifteen other models at Kurlay alone who would dance at the chance to fill my shoes."

"Then let them." He crossed to her and grasped her arms. "Do you understand about Karma?"

"Yes." She didn't look at him. "That's what Sebastian's class lectures are about."

"Then you realize what cause and effect means. But think about influence and result. By doing these advertisements, you're encouraging others to do something you don't believe in. You're involved in a business conspiracy to mold lives. If the results are negative, you're responsible." His grip forced her to look at him.

She squirmed away. "But I'm only the model."

"And a model in an ad is there to be copied. You're a beautiful woman and there are millions of people out there reading magazines and watching television who want to emulate you. You have power. Why not channel your inner, as well as your outer, beauty into something you truly believe in?" He cupped her chin with his hand.

"You're not only beautiful, Jesseree, you're intelligent."

She shook loose of him and crossed to the door. "What do you think I am? Some oracle? I'm just a model, trying to make it out there in a tough business. I'm not ready to be your disciple."

She swirled around. "That's it, isn't it? You want me to do your work."

"My work—your work—it's all the same." He shook his head. "You just can't dismiss it that way. Since you've been here, you have already learned so much. I'm not speaking of right and wrong. I'm referring to what is most natural for your peace of mind."

Until then she'd been working on controlling her anger but now he'd gone too far. "You speak of peace of mind. Maybe you should work on your own." Reaching for the door she pulled it open. "Don't preach, Devon. I'll make my own decisions when I'm ready. And when I do, I'm not going to worry if they meet with your approval." With unseeing eyes, she headed out into the black night. "Just remember." She turned back, the anger making her breath catch. "My spiritual growth is my business. You taught me that."

She crossed the meadow, tripping and stumbling, fighting back tears as she made her way to her cabin. When she reached the porch, she grabbed another log from the pile and barged through the door, kicking it shut behind her. After a fierce stoking up of the coals, she threw the log on top and slammed the metal door. Her head pounded as she reached for her overnight case and searched through it for aspirin.

With trembling fingers, she felt two tablets on the bottom shoved into a corner. She carefully drew them up through the bottles and tubes. Loose Valium. Exactly what she needed. She popped them in her mouth, snatched a cup, and poured water from a jug.

Damn Devon! How dare he attack her about her job? She had struggled a lot of years to go as high as she had near the top of the glamorous ladder. How could she ever expect him to understand? She pulled off her clothes and dropped them in a careless pile. Yanking her gown and robe from a hook behind the door, she pulled the gown over her head and tossed the flannel robe on top of the pile.

Padding across the cold floor, she mumbled her anger until she reached the bed. She climbed into her sleeping bag, punched up her pillow with her fists, and shoved it over her head. As the room grew still, the stove door creaked open, lighting the area around her with a red and yellow glow from the crackling fire within.

Chapter 18

Devon called after her but Jesseree ran out and disappeared into the dark night. Those magazine ads shouldn't have been discussed tonight. After spending the afternoon fasting and meditating, seeking direction on how not to bruise her ego, he had gone ahead and made a mess of things. But when she'd spotted the magazine on his desk, riffled through and questioned him, he felt he had to be honest.

If all of this had waited until tomorrow as he'd planned, he might have been able to handle this situation with tact. His first thought had been to discuss his feelings with Sebastian, but then Jesseree might have been more upset if she thought he went behind her back.

He paced the cabin floor. If he could only make it

clear, her future had become important to him. He wanted to help her make decisions in her work that would bring her peace. His intentions were good. His heart was sincere, but communicating his feelings in a non-threatening manner continued to be a major problem for him.

He sat down and opened his book, but her face crowded his thoughts. When she was angry, her green eyes flashed and her hair danced around her head like cosmic wings, stirring strong emotions he hadn't known existed. When she stood near, physical yearnings washed over his senses, arousing him, and he desired to hold her.

There'd never been a woman to arouse him that way before. Maybe once when he attended the university. A classmate. A student from England. But at the end of the semester, she left him and ran off with another student to live on a farm in Wisconsin, leaving Devon feeling abandoned. After that incident, he threw himself into his studies, then his work here. Yet somewhere deep inside, he had always known his spiritual development could never be complete without a soulmate. The one woman who would share his life.

He dismally thought about the brothers in the Himalayas. Ironically, his chaste life helped make him eligible for that post. But now these feelings for Jesseree complicated things. Reaching for one of the magazines, *THE RUNWAY*, he turned it over to the back cover and studied the full page picture of Jesseree lying on a plush fur rug holding up a martini. If he could point out the negatives in this picture in a loving way, let her see all the objects in the ad that she herself disapproved of, then perhaps she might understand his intent to help her. Realize that he really cared.

He opened the cabin door and looked at the crescent moon as it rose over the mountains. He stepped out and peered through the dark night at Jesseree's cabin. Smoke streamed from the chimney and a faint light flickered at the window. A candle? His thoughts returned to that late afternoon he'd visited her when she'd been cabin-bound with poison oak, remembering how they had sipped tea and burned a candle at twilight. That evening had been the turning point for him. That night he knew he really cared about her.

He stepped back in and picked up his book. After adjusting the lampshade on his desk, he lay down on the bed to read. He must study the Upanishads tonight and outline passages for his morning class.

Mind is indeed the source of bondage. He studied the words carefully. And also the source of liberation. To be bound to things of the world—this is bondage. And also the source of liberation. To be free from them—this is liberation.

He repeated the words softly to himself then closed his eyes. He fell asleep with the Sanskrit Treatises spread across his chest.

ೞೞೞ

The sounds of loud voices and pounding feet outside his window wrenched him from a deep sleep. He lay still a moment before he jumped from his bed and ran to the door. A tower of orange smoke billowed skyward from Jesseree's cabin. Figures raced back and forth across the meadow with hoses and buckets. Grabbing the quilt from his bed, he dashed across the clearing while Ana's shouts for more water echoed across the ashram.

John and Kapula raced ahead of him carrying metal crates. They reached the cabin and smashed them against the window shattering the glass. Billows of black smoke poured from the open window driving them back. Devon ran up alongside them as they plunged through the smoke holding their arms against their faces. They climbed into the inferno and grabbed Jesseree from her bed, motioning Devon to stay outside as they lifted her though the window.

He took her from them, wrapped her in the quilt and rushed away from the smoke and flames to the clearing as showers of water from the hoses soaked his back.

"It's catching the lower branches," Sebastian hollered, grabbing a hose from Manu and turning it on full force. "If it spreads to the forest, we won't be able to control it."

Mary raced after Devon and helped lay Jesseree on the grass. "Oh, dear God," she cried. "Is she breathing?"

She put her ear to Jesseree's mouth while she felt her neck for a pulse. The roar of the fire made it difficult.

When she looked up her eyes filled with fear. "There's a pulse," she screamed. "But I can't tell if she's breathing."

He pinched Jesseree's nose and arched her neck. Covering her mouth with his, he puffed his breath into her smoke filled lungs. Repeatedly and rhythmically, he poured his *prana*, his life force, into her body until she gasped and coughed convulsively.

Leaning close to her wet face, he muttered, "Thank God."

Mary bent down, holding Jesseree's head while Devon kneeled and folded the top of the quilt into a pillow.

"I'll get something for her circulation." Mary skirted around him and ran across the grass.

Anasuya ran up as Mary left. "Is she all right? Can I help?"

"She's breathing," he said, relieved. "I'll keep her here for now. I'll call if I need you."

Ana reached down and felt Jesseree's brow. "She's so cold."

"It's from the water. Don't worry. I'll take care of her."

Ana stood motionless for a moment then darted back to help the men.

When they were alone, Devon carefully lifted Jesseree onto his lap brushing her wet hair from her face. He outlined her cheekbones with his fingers as the fire shot up to the sky creating dark shadows, tinting the grass around them crimson. He put his arms around her and pulled her tightly to him. His cheek pressed against hers.

"Devon?" Her voice weak, she opened her eyes.

"I'm here. You're safe."

She looked toward her cabin and tried to sit up. "What happened?"

"Don't worry about it now," he whispered. "You're with me." He rocked her like a child, cradling her in his arms. She closed her eyes and her head fell against his chest. Leaning over, he covered her mouth with his, this time tenderly. His lips moved up to her eyelids. When she stirred, he buried his face in her hair. "I love you, Jesseree," he whispered. "Jesseree—Jewel of Desire."

Mary ran up out of breath clutching her bag and basket. "How is she?"

He stood and held Jesseree in his arms while he carefully pulled the quilt around her. "Let's take her to my cabin."

As they crossed the clearing, he looked back just in time to see the remains of her cabin collapse into relentless flames.

✧✧✧

The next morning, Jesseree awoke and peered through slitted eyes to the old brown trunk in the corner. She turned slowly onto her side and her hair tumbled across her face, filling her nostrils with the acrid smell of smoke. She cringed and clutched at the pain in her chest. Why was she here in Devon's cabin? She swallowed hard against her raw throat. How did she get here? She flashed on last night then flinched as she recalled her cabin in flames. She sat upright. "Devon?"

Ana jumped up from the chair. "Jess, you're awake. How do you feel?"

"Why am I here?" Her voice came out in a hoarse whisper. She held her throat." Where's Devon?"

Ana hesitated. "There was an accident. A fire. Oh, Jess. I was so scared for you." She reached down and gave her a hug. "No one let me know that they'd gotten you out of the cabin until I saw you in the clearing with Devon. I was afraid you were dead."

Jesseree patted Ana's back. "I'm all right, I guess. How did it happen?"

"We don't know," Ana searched Jesseree's face. "I went out to use the bathroom and saw the flames. I screamed for the others."

Jesseree gasped. "Anyone hurt?"

"No. Thank God." Ana's eyes misted as she kissed Jesseree on the brow.

Jesseree tried to recall what happened but most of it was a blur. She remembered leaving Devon's cabin in a rage then throwing a log in the stove. She had slammed the stove door.

But did she pull the handle down? And her clothes! She'd left them piled on the floor.

Holding her head she groaned. "Ana, are you sure everyone's all right? No one's hurt?"

Ana nodded. "It was awful. Really frightening. Everyone worked together to put out the fire. And most important, you're safe."

Jesseree patted the quilt. "How did I get here?"

"Devon and Mary carried you. He stayed up all night watching after you. At daylight he asked if I would take his place when he left for Shasta."

"He's gone?"

"Paul's lecturing up there today. Devon packed his bag and joined him. He said you can stay here in his cabin. When he gets back, you can stay with me if you want."

Overwhelmed with guilt, Jesseree felt like crying. She could think of only one logical explanation for the fire. In her anger, she'd taken those pills and forgotten to shove the handle down tight on the stove door, as Ana had stressed that first morning.

Ana lifted a bag and set it on the bed. "All your things were destroyed. I brought this skirt and blouse for you to wear." She held the blouse up. "I hope they fit. And there's a pair of Mary's sandals in the bag. She sends them with her love." She bustled around the room straightening the furniture before she left. "I promise to be back when I'm finished in the kitchen."

Jesseree got up, dressed in Ana's clothes and then stood in the doorway looking at the rubble that had been her cabin. She coughed and winced, remembering the smoke and flames. She walked out across the clearing wearing one of Devon's heavy sweaters with the collar pulled up around her ears. The cold grass, still heavy with water, soaked her feet. When she reached the burned-out site, she stood staring and shivering. Nothing left of her cabin except pieces of charred wood strewn around the ground. Above her head a pine tree's blackened limbs hung dangerously low.

Dear Lord! Her negligence could have set the forest on fire. Everyone here at Ahimsa took special care that this would never happen. She came here as a guest and almost destroyed all that they'd struggled to build. Tears of regret and shame slid down her cheeks at the thought of facing the others. If only they'd reprimand her, but she knew they wouldn't. They were all too kind.

Lost in her dreary thoughts, she didn't see the figure crossing the meadow. She started when a warm hand rested on her shoulder.

"I'm glad to see you're up, Jess," Sebastian said pleasantly. "We were all worried about you, but Devon chose to keep a vigil at the cabin last night so the rest of us could sleep. Come join me in the dining room for breakfast. Everyone is waiting to see you."

His kindness didn't surprise her. She had expected it. But hearing his voice made her weep. Sebastian reached out and held her. When her sobs subsided, he placed a handkerchief in her hand and an arm around her shoulders. "Come," he said gently and guided her up to the white house.

Chapter 19

Paul put down his notes, rolled down his window, and looked over at Devon. "We've been on the road for three hours and you haven't said a word. What's going on with you? If it's about the fire, stop worrying. It's over and done with minimum damage. Be thankful that everyone at our place is safe."

Devon kept his eyes on the road. "I caused that fire."

Paul squinted. "What are you talking about? The flames came from Jesseree's cabin. The consensus is that her stove door wasn't closed tight and some clothing in her place caught a hot coal."

"That may be. But she went to bed upset and I'm the one who caused it."

"You upset her? Why?"

Devon shook his head. "I got up on my holier-than-thou platform and didn't let up. Once again, I attempted to force my thoughts and feelings on another—this time on a fine, lovely…"

Paul waited but Devon closed up again. He hesitated, and rubbed his chin, "Okay. So you're into Jesseree emotionally. Not just her instructor now? There has been some gossip around the grounds but I didn't take much stock in what folks were saying."

Devon shot him a sidelong look.

"Okay." Paul folded his hands. "I get it. Enough!" He checked his papers. "How are we doing with the lecture? Did you want to add anything after my talk? I figure my notes should cover almost all of the hour on nuclear freeze, but I can cut it short if you need to answer questions. Answering is not my thing. Extemporaneous never worked well for me." His brows knit into a questioning frown. "Are you planning to sit up on the stage?"

"Originally, that was the plan. But it's changed. You'll do fine, Paul. I'll stay until you get started then come back to pick you up. My old instructor from Berkley will be the moderator. I called him. He'll be there to take questions. The meeting should last about two hours. Potluck will be served when the meeting lets out."

Paul gave him a side glance. "You're okay, right?"

Devon tapped the steering wheel. "I'm good. I need to sort through plans that I've made in the past and I need a quiet space to do that. I'll be heading for the foot of

Mount Shasta. There might be snow. But that won't stop me. I'll walk the paths. I came here eight years ago when I was at odds with myself. I left renewed." He didn't add that at that time he met a man—and he hoped to meet him again. When Jess had confided to him about the white-robed monk on Eagle's Point, it had brought back the memory of the person he'd met here in Shasta. At the time Devon figured the man who spoke to him lived nearby. Perhaps in a cabin Strange though, meeting him back then had given him the strength to work through his problem. But strangely, he'd left the mountain with no memory of what their conversation had been about.

Now in retrospect, he wasn't too sure there had even been a conversation. Although there were times bits and pieces of that meeting came to him in his dreams. Nothing tangible. Swirling clouds and echoing voices of men and women chanting. When he had those dreams—not often, but somewhat vivid—he always awoke with a start.

After he'd left this region, he searched city bookstores and found American Indian legends of Mount Shasta. In another book written in the 1880s, there was a mention of Mu, a lost continent, the first recorded continent off the coast of North America flooded 12,000 years ago and submerged on the ocean floor. All that was left of that continent were the tops of volcanoes jutting up into the Pacific Ocean forming the inhabited islands we are familiar with now.

What had really interested him at the time was reading of a hidden city of advanced beings, survivors of Mu, living in or on Mount Shasta who established a secret colony. In his literary search back then, he'd found a number of myths and legends. This one in particular had fascinated him. Could there possibly be a city beneath the mountain peaks in a complex of tunnels? A secret colony preserving their ancient customs? In some of the legends the city was no longer inhabited, while in others he read that it was inhabited by a technological advanced society of humans that were occasionally seen walking the surface dressed in loose flowing clothes. Had he been in contact with a survivor?

In his busy lifestyle at Ahimsa and his numerous lecturing tours, he'd put most of what he had studied at that time on the back burner. But Jesseree's experience on Eagle's Point had given him a mental and emotional tug. Now eight years later, he would be revisiting the mountain, but try as he could, he was unable to recall what had transpired years ago. One thing he knew for sure, after leaving the man and the mountain, his lectures for planet peace had advanced to the level of where he and Paul were able to lecture now.

Paul pointed out a road sign. "We're almost there." He checked his watch. "Twenty more miles."

He gathered his papers and placed them in his folder. The two men remained quiet, Devon lost in thought for the next half-hour, until arrowed signs led them into the small town of Shasta.

After Devon helped Paul out of the passenger seat into his chair, he wheeled him into the meeting, a grand room decorated with black and white posters and colorful pamphlets supporting-their cause. Devon shook hands with his old professor and left the hall impatient to reach the mountain.

An hour later, after driving a winding road, he stood near the bottom of the 14,000-foot volcano, and found himself surrounded in natural beauty. Devon walked from the car, slowed his pace, relaxed his shoulders, and took a deep breath. The tension he'd been feeling on the trip here slowly evaporated. A cold wind passed by and he zipped up his jacket before he started the climb on the path that would eventually rise up to the rim. Someday he hoped to make that climb to the summit. But not today.

He hadn't gone too far when he looked up to see someone approaching, coming down the path. As the person drew closer, Devon could see it was a man. An extremely tall man, possibly close to seven feet. The man raised his arm and waved. Devon stopped and waited for the man to join him.

ↄ∂ↄↄ

Two hours later, Devon met up with Paul at the meeting hall.

"I snagged a sandwich from the potluck," Paul said. "Hope you like egg salad."

When they were both settled in the car, Devon carefully set the sandwich in the glovebox.

Paul frowned. "What? Not hungry? Did you grab something to eat in town?"

Devon shook his head. "No. I'm not hungry. The truth? I feel uncomfortably full."

"Of what?" Paul narrowed his eyes. "Did something happen when you were at the mountain?"

"Yes. Something did happen. Or I felt it did. It's difficult to explain."

As they headed to Chico College for their next speaking engagement on their agenda, Devon tried again. "I met up with a person. At first, I thought maybe it was the same person I had met over eight years ago. He looked the same. But I found it strange he hadn't aged."

Paul wiggled around and adjusted his seat belt while Devon went on to describe his first meeting on the mountain eight years ago.

"Could be the same man," Paul said. "Or not. Describe him."

"Extremely tall, thin, maybe a hundred and sixty pounds. Long neck as compared to us. A broad nose." Devon hesitated. "His eyes—large and clear. His hair—fair and curly. A prominent forehead—unusually high. He wore a blue robe and sandals. When he reached me, he raised his hand in greeting. I don't know how he knew my name, but he spoke it in English tinged with a British accent."

"Maybe he's related to the first guy you met there. A cousin or brother."

"Could be. He said he was an archeologist. But that doesn't explain how he knew my name."

"Did you ask where he lives?"

"No." Devon squinted. "After the first few minutes, I don't recall asking him anything. And this is the strange part. I don't believe I even spoke. When he approached me, I felt like I was standing in some sort of a mist. I could see his lips moving but now I can't tell you what he said." Devon pulled over to the side of the road and faced Paul. "Except when I turned to leave."

"Yeah? What?"

"He placed his hand on my shoulder and there was an echo to his voice that made it sound like a proclamation. 'Follow your heart,' he said. 'You will accomplish all that you were sent here to do to complete the task. No matter what your decision, there will be consequences.' He held out his hand. 'Take this.'" Devon reached into his jacket pocket and brought out a small blue velvet bag. He opened it and reached in with his finger and pulled out a gold nugget.

"He gave you gold?" Paul's eyes widened. "Let me see it."

Devon handed it over. "He gave me the nugget and this leather pouch. It's filled with gold dust."

Paul leaned back and huffed. "That's fantastic. So what do you make of it?'

Devon slowly shook his head.

Paul lifted a brow and smiled. "Well, for what it's worth, I spoke to a woman after the lecture today, a really pretty lady, by the way. Name's Corrine. She gave me her number and wants to keep in touch. I spoke about our upcoming festival at Ahimsa and she'd like to attend. Anyway, she lives here in the town of Shasta. Grew up here. When I mentioned I was waiting for you to come back from the mountain, her interest peaked and she asked why you had gone there. I told her about your experience at the foot of the mountain eight years ago. Corrine nodded knowingly and told me a number of the locals here have had experiences with the people that live on the mountain and in the surrounding forest."

"Experiences?" Devon's eyes narrowed. "What kind of experiences? Similar to mine?"

"Not exactly." Paul rubbed the nugget with his thumb. "But she did mention these mountain folks do own gold. Seems occasionally when they need some modern commodities, they come to the town stores and pay with gold nuggets and never ask for or accept change. Whenever they are asked questions by curious store owners, they turn away, reluctant to give any information about themselves." Paul eyed Devon's small bag. "Sometimes they pay for their goods with gold dust. At first, townspeople found them strange. Now when they see them walking along the highway in their robes and sandals, they nod. Once in a while, the Shasta Mountain men nod back."

"How about their women? Do they go into town?"

"She didn't say and I didn't ask. But here's another bit of info she told me—whether this is fact or fiction, I don't know—but she swears a couple of times at night she's seen a brilliant white light, kind of a violet blue cast up into the trees, tingeing the edge of a low hanging cloud.

Devon reached over and removed the sandwich from the glove box.

Paul laughed. "Oh, so you're hungry now? Does her story give you an appetite?"

Devon chewed thoughtfully. "Could be. I'm not sure if what your new friend told you is just a story—strange, but it I feels like I've heard some of this before."

Paul nodded. "Well, there's more." He shrugged. "You up for it?"

Devon shrugged and wrapped the remainder of his sandwich in a napkin. "I feel it's important you tell me what she said."

Paul squinted. "Why? Do you believe?"

"I'll put it this way. After what I've experienced at the mountain during both of my visits, I don't disbe-lieve."

"Okay then. This one will rock ya. Last year, her grandmother told her that years ago when she was a child, a very old majestic man of nobility had come out of the mountain and made an important trip by foot over two hundred miles to San Francisco. When he reached there, he was greeted by some wealthy men at the Ferry Building then escorted up to City Hall to a special ceremony where all strangers were forbidden. Who he was or what he went there to do no one in town knows."

"Did he stay in the city?

"Her grandmother didn't say. But she said in the past there were similar stories told about strange individuals from around here."

Devon turned the key, started the engine, and wondered if the people that lived in the forests and the mountains of Shasta were the descendants of the submerged continent of Mu.

'Follow your heart. You will accomplish all that you were sent here to do to complete the task. No matter what your decision, there will be consequences.'

Devon gazed out the windshield at the white line dividing the road ahead. Perhaps, he thought to himself, my task is not the Himalayas but to be with Jesseree for the rest of our lives.

Chapter 20

Karen Kelso stopped under the purple awning of the Union Street Cafe to catch her breath and close her umbrella. What was so damn important that she had to meet Jacob during her lunch hour? Mumbling her annoyance, she stomped the water off her open toe pumps.

She searched the street for his BMW. He better have it parked close by because she wasn't walking back to work in this rain. He'd called her at a busy time at the bank, when she didn't have time to talk, or she would have insisted he pick her up.

After brushing off the moisture gathered on the shoulders of her beige raincoat, she straightened her hair. What a shocker hearing from him today. He was the last person she cared to see but there had been urgency in his voice. If he wasn't her cousin she would have refused. Especially in the rain.

She pushed through the carved door of Luchi's Italian restaurant, and stepped inside. A long line of people bunched up ahead of her, but she instantly spotted Jacob sitting in a booth at the rear of the long room. He saw her and waved.

"Hello, Jacob," she called as she passed him to hang her coat on a brass coatrack. "What's happening?"

He was crouched in the booth next to the wall and his hair was soaked.

She came back and sat across from him. "Okay. What's so important?" She glanced at her watch. "I have to be back at the bank at one."

He looked up at her from his wine glass. "You want a drink?"

"No thanks." The waitress came and Karen ordered a salad. She glanced over at him. "Are you paying?"

When he nodded, she said, "Good. I'll have a slice of cherry cheesecake too." When the waitress left, Karen smiled wickedly. "I'm dieting as usual. But they have the greatest desserts here. What did you order?

"Nothing," he muttered. "I'm not hungry." He leaned forward across the table.

Karen sniffed. His tweed jacket, wet and wrinkled, smelled dirty and he needed a shave.

Oh, oh, Karen thought as she looked into his watery

eyes. He's drunk. She didn't have time for this. Forget about having him drive her back to work. She'd eat and run.

It was really hard for her to think of Jacob as a lush. But that's what he was turning into. They had been so close in high school. Only lived a mile apart in Marin. Jacob had been president of their junior class, and all of her girlfriends were wild about him. He also excelled on the debating team, and she'd been proud to call him cousin.

The family was convinced that he took after her father and that someday Jacob would become a criminal attorney too. But the years passed and people changed and she really didn't like him anymore. He'd made such an ass of himself last year at the family Christmas party. Making cruel jokes about everyone, and especially her dad who had done so much to help him.

She felt sorry for her Aunt Shirley. Always making excuses for him. Always worrying about him. It was just family gossip, but she'd heard that now Shirley was drinking, too. What a shame. At one time, they'd all been so close.

Now as she sat across from him she studied his face. "Lord, you look awful," She sniffed. "How come you're not in class today?"

He ran his fingers through his damp hair. "Forget the questions," he snapped. "I need your help."

The waitress came back with the salad and Karen

dug in. She avoided Jacob's eyes. If he wanted money, she didn't have any to loan and she'd tell him so. A single working girl living alone in the city never had extra bucks. Even if she did, she wouldn't give it to him. He'd just waste it on booze.

"I need an address," he whispered. "And you can get it for me."

Karen narrowed her eyes and took a sip of water. "Why are you whispering?"

"You can get it at the bank."

She crunched on the ice from her glass. Man, he sounded weird. "Jacob, why are you whispering? I can hardly hear you. If you've got something to say, spit it out."

He moved closer to the table and cupped his mouth with his stained fingers. "I said I want you to get an address for me."

She was getting irritated with his mysterious antics. "Whose is it?"

"She's a customer at the bank. I need her forwarding address."

Karen dropped her fork. "Are you insane? I can't give out information like that." She snickered at him then began eating again. Next he'd want the customer's phone number.

"I'm not fooling around, Karen. I need that information."

His tone caused her to look up. Dark eyes glowed

ominously back at her. "Look, Jacob. I'm not going to sit here and listen to your demands." She stood, patted her mouth with a corner of the napkin, and reached for her purse. "Tell the waitress to forget the cheesecake. I'm going to try to forget that we had this conversation. I'm too busy to put up with this crap."

"Sit down," he shouted. Customers and two waitresses turned and stared.

Stunned, Karen sat.

"Now. Just stay there until I'm finished. I want the forwarding address of Jesseree Lipton." He lowered his voice. "I know she has an account at your bank."

She was too shocked to speak. He'd never treated her like this before even at the Christmas party. When she left here, she most certainly would call his mother.

"Do as I ask, Karen," he warned. "Or you'll regret it."

She swallowed hard as the blood surged on the sides of her neck. She decided to reason with him. "I can't give out information like that. I'll lose my job."

He relaxed and leaned back looping his thumbs in the waist of his Levis. "Remember when we were seniors, Karen?" His voice turned chummy and cold. "Remember when you needed my help?"

She paled and searched his face. Her thoughts raced back to a black time in her young life. Not that! He wouldn't. That was the only time she'd gone to anyone except her parents when she needed help. But at that time she couldn't turn to them. Her father would never have understood. So she'd gone to Jacob.

Seventeen and pregnant, she needed an abortion. It seemed the only way out to her then. Jacob had gone to Planned Parenthood with her and had helped her choose a doctor. "Don't worry," he told her back then, squeezing her arm. "No one will ever know." He'd been like a rock, helping her through a difficult time. When it was over and done, he promised that they would never talk about it again. And they hadn't—until now.

"Karen," he said impatiently. "Are you going to get what I want or should I have a little chat with your dad?"

Her eyes filled with tears. "If they find out at the bank, I'll lose my job."

"Well, take your pick, cuz."

His darkness encompassed their booth shutting out all noise from the surrounding tables while his negative energy sealed them together. She realized there would be no escape until she gave him her answer.

Chapter 21

Jesseree pulled into the driveway of the brown brick house in Grass Valley. She smiled at the sight of her dear friend Sarah standing on the porch in a blue cashmere sweater, her graying hair wound around her head in a lovely thick braid. Jesseree waved to her from the car window and Sarah waved back as she stepped lightly down the steps to the stone walkway. Jesseree rushed from the car to greet her. They hugged.

"You look wonderful." Sarah guided Jesseree over to a redwood bench next to a small reflecting pond. She examined her with maternal eyes. "I don't have to ask how you've been. It shows. You've gained weight and your color is good." She traced the curve of Jesseree's face. "It's grand to see you."

Jesseree basked in the light of Sarah's affection. "I have really missed you, but I've felt you near me so many times since I've been gone."

Sarah smiled warmly. "That's because our souls are in tune."

Jesseree glanced around. "How long will you be staying here? Where are the people who own this house?"

"The Helfers? James and Rosemary. Would you believe they've gone to visit your grandmother in Sedona? They're old friends of your grandma and me. I'm housesitting while they're away. This town is on my way to Ahimsa for the Indian Feast so it's working out fine."

She slowly appraised Jesseree's clothes. "Looks like you're dressing like the other resident women at the retreat now."

Jesseree looked down at her skirt. "Not really. These clothes aren't mine. They belong to Ana and Mary. The sweater's Devon's." She wondered if Sarah knew about the fire. "I do need to go shopping this afternoon for some new duds. Will you join me?"

On the way to the shopping center, Jesseree told Sarah about the fire. "The carpenters are already at Ahimsa helping John rebuild the cabin. I called the bank in San Francisco and made arrangements for the funds to be sent directly to Sebastian. He refused to take the money at first, but I threatened to leave if he didn't. He finally agreed, but only as a love offering. If I had been negligent, he said, then so be it. We all make mistakes."

Sarah nodded. "Sebastian believes that it's people not things that are important. And he's right. You were safe. That's all that mattered."

"What bothers me, Sarah, is that I took two Valium before I went to bed. If I hadn't passed out, maybe I would have smelled the smoke in time to save the cabin."

Sarah looked concerned. "Do you still find it necessary to take pills in order to sleep?"

"I took Valium when I was in the city, but I haven't had to use them at the retreat. I didn't think I had any with me." She glanced sideways at Sarah. "I found them buried in my bag and swallowed them because I was angry with Devon."

They entered the parking area. Sarah waited until Jesseree turned off the motor. "Don't you and Devon get along?"

"Most of the time. It took a while for us to become friends.

"We don't have to talk about it if you're not comfortable." Sarah opened the car door and stepped out.

"But I do want to." Jesseree climbed out on her side. "It's crazy but I think I love him."

"Well. That's good news." She covered Jesseree's hand with her own. "When we get your shopping done, we'll have a nice long chat."

∽∾∽

Back at the house Sarah folded the shopping bags.

"Do you have enough things now until you get back to the city?"

Jesseree nodded as she slipped on her new down jacket.

"I like that color on you," Sarah said. "Pink is the color of love."

Jesseree slipped out of her coat then sat down in the kitchen.

Sarah eased herself into the chair across from her. "Now what's all this about you and Devon?"

"I don't know if it's about me and Devon. It might just be about me." She told Sarah how angry she'd become when he tried to talk to her about the magazine ads. But now since she'd had time to think things through, she'd come to realize that he was right about a lot of things. "That's why I agreed to go to Ahimsa in the first place. I wanted peace. But when he criticized those pictures, my work, I just couldn't take it. My strong ego, I guess."

"So now what?"

"I'm not sure. I know that some modeling jobs have caused me a lot of anxiety—and guilt. When I don't believe in a product I'm paid to advertise, I get uptight, then I start to think about something else I'd rather be doing and block it out. That's what's known as denial."

"Did you feel that Devon tried to tell you what to do?"

"I suppose. He can get bossy."

Sarah laughed knowingly. "Yes. But you're his student and he speaks to you as a teacher. He feels a responsibility. He may not be the most tactful man but you usually know where you stand."

The phone rang and Sarah left to answer. When she returned she put cookies on a plate. "That was the Helfers. They'll be back tomorrow."

"Great news." Jesseree smiled. "Now we can drive back to Ahimsa together."

Sarah nodded. "Good. I'll be able to help you and Ana with the preparations for the Indian Feast."

Jesseree had forgotten about the Indian Feast. Her concern over the fire and making arrangements to have the cabin rebuilt had taken up most of her time. "Wow. That's next week."

"Right," Sarah added, "I'd like to show you what I brought with me to wear that night." She hurried down the hall and when she came back she held a long white box in her arms. "I always wear the same costume every year, and I have one for you too if you're interested. She reached in the box and pulled out two Indian saris with veils.

Jesseree rushed over. "They're gorgeous. Where did you get this material?"

"In India. The year you were born.

Jesseree immediately wrapped one of the silks around her. "Is this the way you wear it?"

"Not quite. There's a real knack to the draping, it's a

bit complicated, to do it now, but I'll help you on the night of the party."

Jesseree went into the living room holding the rich fabric under her chin and stood there gazing at her reflection in the mirror over the fireplace.

"This green is absolutely fabulous. I've seen this shade before." She narrowed her eyes. "I had a dream I was wearing this exact color." She nodded. "Emerald green." She folded the material and placed it back in the box. "So you were in India. Did you know Devon is planning to go to the Himalayas?"

Sarah clapped her hands. "That's wonderful. Then he's been accepted?"

"Yes. But he says he can't go."

Sarah came around the table and faced her. "Why not?"

"Personal reasons." Jesseree knew how much Sarah loved him. If she told her why maybe she could help. "It concerns his parents."

Sarah sat down. "Are they ill?"

Jesseree shook her head and leaned against the counter. "Didn't you mention that you knew his father?"

Sarah nodded. "Yes. A friend of mine. A long time ago."

"I don't know if I have the liberty to say, but maybe you can help since you knew his dad. Devon won't accept the position in India because he feels he's not worthy. He can't forgive his father for hurting his mother years ago." Jesseree picked up a cookie and nibbled at the edge before she told the rest of the story to Sarah exactly the way Devon had told it to her. When she came to the part about the blue letter with the signature Star, Sarah held up her hand. "Stop." She clutched at her chest. "Does Devon have the letter?"

Jesseree straightened. "Sarah. What is it?"

The older woman's face drained of color.

"I'm sorry. I don't mean to worry you." Jesseree rushed to her side and knelt on the floor. "We don't need to talk about this."

Sarah stood unsteadily and clung on to Jesseree's arm. "This pain. Had it before. I've been working on it—doing healings. Help me to the chair in the living room."

Jesseree did as Sarah requested and slipped a foot-stool under her feet.

"Don't fuss."

The color slowly returned to Sarah's face. She closed her eyes and leaned her head back against the chair. Jesseree waited by her side until she opened them again. Sarah looked at Jesseree and held out her hand.

"Sit down, dear." Her eyes filled with tears and sadness clouded her face. "I must tell you something."

"What is it?" Jesseree scanned her face. "You know you can tell me anything."

"I'm Star. The woman who wrote that letter to Mathew—Devon's father."

Chapter 22

Jesseree stared at Sarah in disbelief. "You're who? Star? I can't believe it. You're the other woman?"

"It's a long story," Sarah nodded sadly. "And I had no idea that Devon knew."

"He doesn't know much. That's part of the problem. He has no idea of what really happened. His mother never gave him any details and he wouldn't ask his dad."

"But how could his mother have known? What happened between Mathew and me was over a long time before Mathew met Devon's mother."

"This is bizarre." Jesseree raised her hands. "You're the one Devon's been blaming all of these years for the breakup of his family?"

Sarah sighed as she pressed her palm to her forehead.

"That letter was never meant to hurt anyone. I wrote it to Mathew in India to help heal the wound I'd caused him when we were together in San Francisco." The years suddenly fell away from Sarah's face. "A time when we were in love. He came into my life in 1944 when I thought I'd never feel the blood flow through my veins again. A time when I was still raw and bleeding from a War Department Telegram two years earlier informing me that my husband, David, would never come home. That the shores of Corregidor held him forever. I met Mathew one night at the Stage Door Canteen on Market Street. I taught tap dancing at a studio over on Eddy, and that night my teen tap class had been asked to perform for the GIs. Your mother—" She smiled. "—had just turned fourteen and she was my lead dancer. And your grandma, my very best friend, accompanied us on the piano." Sarah nodded in rhythm while she hummed a few bars of "The Boogie Woogie Bugle Boy from Company B."

Jesseree sat down and leaned forward, not wanting to miss a word of this story.

"Before the war, my husband and I were a dance team," Sarah continued. "Vaudeville, you know. But when David left to fight in the Pacific, rather than go on as a single act, I started a dance studio on Eddy Street. I rented two flats. The ground floor was a dance studio and I lived in the flat upstairs." She gazed across the room immersed in memories. "It's strange how souls can pass each other in this lifetime and be unaware of the bond between them. Who back then could have predicted that one day Louise's daughter, you, and Mathew's son, Devon, would be together at a mountain retreat helping each other untangle their lives?

Jesseree nodded thoughtfully.

"That night at the canteen when Mathew strolled over to compliment the girls on their dancing, he looked handsome as a Hollywood movie star in his naval officer's uniform. He complimented the kids on their dance numbers and asked to meet their teacher. When he introduced himself, something in his hazel eyes fanned embers deep inside me. Embers that I thought had died with David." Sarah paused as if to savor the magic of that moment.

In the silence, Jesseree tried to imagine the scene. Sarah, blonde, wearing shoulder pads and a pompadour. Grandma, a true redhead, thumping boogie on the piano. Her mother, Louise, in a satin red, white, and blue patriotic costume. And Mathew—if he'd been as handsome as Devon, he must have been a knockout.

"We spent the rest of that first evening together. Mathew and I danced to the jukebox then talked over coffee and donuts for hours. When he asked if I would see him the next night, I accepted. I was thirty-six." She smiled again. "And he was twenty-four. I told him later that he'd been bewitched by an older woman. He insisted that wasn't true, that he would have fallen for me no matter what. He was a Navy pilot waiting on Treasure Island for reassignment after his carrier had gone down near Iwo Jima. We spent a lifetime together in those three weeks. He was so different from David—and yet…" Her eyes filled with tears. She stopped and wiped them with a hanky. "My life with David had revolved around our careers. We chose not to have children. Too busy working toward the Big Time. He became my child, and I became his. We took care of each other. That's all we needed."

Her voice trembled. "When David didn't return to me, I met and held on to Mathew. His strong arms eased some of my heartache. He brightened the darkness of the war and covered me with his youth—and his warmth— and all the other strengths a man offers a woman he loves. I hungrily seized it all. I gave back nothing. Nothing but the heartache of my refusal to marry him." Sarah's chin tilted upward and Jesseree felt a veil fall between them. "You see?" she continued as if explaining her actions beyond the room. "I viewed my career as my future. Television was new and New York put together the first musical comedy. I wanted to choreograph. This shattered Mathew when I shared my dream. I tried to reason with him, convince him his whole life lay ahead for him. He already had earned his Civil Engineering Degree. The post war world would be his oyster. Oh yes, my feelings for him were strong. He'd made me feel alive again, desirable. But that wasn't strong enough to make me change my mind."

She shook her head slowly. Her face clouded and she

asked Jesseree for a glass of water. When Jesseree returned, Sarah sipped from the glass. "When Mathew came to me that last night, his eyes were pools of sorrow. 'I've been reassigned. Please wait for me—be here when I get back.' He wept when I told him this was goodbye. I cried too. We held each other all through the night like two scared children. Later, as he dressed in the foggy light of dawn, for just an instant I saw David's eyes sparkling through Mathew's shadowed face and I understood why I had made my decision. It was made out of fear. There would be no more promises to loves that never returned. No more telegrams, 'We regret to inform you…' Printed words to numb my thoughts, my heart and my life. It was easier to seal that short lifetime Mathew and I had shared into a golden pocket of my mind. Golden times that enemy forces and power-hungry governments could never touch. That morning I watched Mathew disappear down the wet vacant City streets below my window. When I heard a cab door slam, my heart shattered."

Sarah wiped her eyes again and again. Jesseree waited through another long silence while Sarah struggled for her voice. "After that he wrote every month for a year. But I didn't answer. I never saw him again—until one night in India."

She stood and Jesseree supported her as she crossed to a table and switched on a lamp. The light instantly flooded the room with the present, but Sarah remained in the past. "When the war ended, I left for New York to offer my talent to a medium that didn't want it. But I stayed on, struggling for my one big break. I most certainly had the experience to teach and perform. I was good but the competition was fierce. Two years later, I returned to San Francisco defeated and broke. An ageing dancer in a world filled with new young artists. I applied for a position at UC Berkeley as an instructor of modern dance and got it.

"While I worked at the college, I studied comparative religions hoping to understand what the war had been all about. That's when I met Sebastian seeking answers too. After a few years, I took a sabbatical and went to India, still searching. One afternoon I attended a tea at the American Embassy in Delhi and Mathew was there with his wife and child, little Devon, a toddler, barely three. After the war Mathew had taken a position with an English construction company building railroads across India. When I spotted him across the room, old feelings surfaced and that afternoon, I desperately regretted letting him go. I got up and left, went outside, but he found me on the terrace. He held his baby by the hand. Beautiful Devon. A dark copy of his fair father.

"Mathew insisted I see him later at my hotel. Not wanting to cause a scene, I agreed. But when I looked down into the innocent eyes of that beautiful child, I knew I could never keep that promise. Later when Mathew arrived at the hotel, I had gone. Only a letter of explanation waited for him. A letter written on blue stationary, filled with my love, telling him of the deep regret I had for not sharing my life with him.

"I explained that I had been a vain selfish woman interested in personal success when the greatest success I could have had on this earth would have been to be the mother of our child. I signed the letter Star—Mathew's love name for me. I didn't have to make it in television to achieve that status with him."

Sarah became silent. Jesseree leaned against the stone fireplace and observed her. Sarah's face had changed into many expressions as she relived the past. Now her expression appeared relaxed.

"Those were my feelings then," she said. "And with the awareness I have now years later, I realize that I had no contract in this incarnation to have children. Mathew did, however. If indeed we were together in some former life, and I believe we were, then maybe that part of my karma with him was fulfilled. Yet it's strange. There are times when I feel Devon is my son, even though I'm not his biological mother." While Jesseree remained silent, trying to process all of this startling information about people and family she thought she knew, Sarah began again. "Sixteen years later when Sebastian and Devon came to my home in Sausalito, you can imagine my surprise when Devon introduced himself. By then I'd retired as a dance instructor and I taught metaphysics in my home. When I learned that other young people from Berkeley were working toward peace, I let them move to the land David and I had bought before the war. They worked hard to pay off the mortgage and—well, you know the rest. Ahimsa, their brotherhood retreat, has been a huge success."

"That is really some love story." Jesseree hesitated. "I suppose Mathew never stopped caring for you."

Sarah's face flushed. "I know I still love him. I don't believe we ever stop loving souls that have been part of our lives. When they're gone, the pain of separation eventually leaves our heart but the love there remains forever."

"When Devon came to your house, were you ever tempted to tell him about his father?"

"At that time, he was still distressed over his mother. I had no idea why she had left and I didn't feel at liberty to discuss the past with him."

"And now?"

Sarah looked thoughtful. "I'll meditate and listen for direction."

The next morning, Jesseree and Sarah packed the back of Jesseree's sports car with their bags while the Helfers trailed behind them, chattering on about Alice in Sedona. "She sends her love to both of you, and she wants to hear what you two are up to."

Sarah and Jesseree exchanged knowing smiles as they thanked them for the message. The two women climbed into the car and waved as they backed out of the driveway.

On the hour drive back up to Ahimsa, Jesseree told Sarah about the Downieville incident and the monk on the plateau. Sarah said she felt that all of Jesseree's visions were leading up to something very important and perhaps revealing. "It seems you're being led. Just be patient and see what happens."

Jesseree brought up Devon. Said she missed him desperately. More than she ever thought she would. His face shone from everyone she encountered. From the checker at the market where they stopped to pick up snacks, to the service station attendant when they pulled in for gas. A couple of times she thought she heard his voice. Each time she turned hoping to see his face, there was no one there. Headed up Highway 49, a car passed them and she thought Devon was driving. She sped up to see. Foolish. He must still be in Shasta. A warm glow spread through her at the thought of seeing him again. She would immediately tell him that her job was now open for debate, and that after thinking things through, she could see his point and agreed on some issues he had brought up. She would also apologize for causing the destructive fire.

When they approached Glory Road, Jesseree slowed to make the turn. Sarah let out a small happy cry. "I get so excited when I come here." She squirmed in her seat. "It will be good to see all my old friends together again."

The car moved slowly up the rutted road. When they reached the steepest slope, Jesseree geared down. "This road will be graded before next week. Sebastian's expecting quite a crowd for the peace sessions. Devon and Paul are picking up a guest speaker in San Francisco from West Germany. Seems he has pertinent information to share."

"It's all so grand," Sarah said. "There will be people travelling here from Light Centers all over this country, and now we'll hear first-hand news of the progress being made in Europe."

As they pulled into the parking area, Jesseree spotted Paul rolling his chair down the path toward the greenhouse. "They're back." She squeezed Sarah's hand. "Devon's here."

Chapter 23

Devon looked up when Sarah called his name. "What a great surprise." He jumped up from a rattan chair on the white house porch and met them at the foot of the steps. "I've missed you both." He reached for Sarah's bag and gave her a warm hug. "And Jesseree." He greeted her with a friendly arm around her shoulders. "Let's take Sarah's things upstairs."

Upstairs of the main house consisted of two dormitories. Women's on the east, directly over the kitchen. The men's, over the office on the west.

"There's not much privacy here," Jesseree commented as she glanced around at the eight dormitory beds. "Wouldn't you be more comfortable with us in Ana's cabin?"

"No." Sarah shook her head. "By the weekend this room will be buzzing." She dropped her purse on a wrought iron bed, the one closest to the front window. "At home, I have privacy. Here I want to mingle." She sat down in a wicker chair. "This is my favorite spot." She pointed out the window. "From here I have a view of Eagle's Point."

Jesseree and Devon followed her over and sat on the edge of the bed.

Sarah turned to Devon. "How did your lectures go in Shasta? Are people turning out?"

"More than we expected. Many signed up to come here for the celebration." He turned and faced Jesseree. "It's been a long two weeks but we accomplished a lot." He smiled knowingly. "There's also been a healing in my personal life."

For a moment Jesseree thought he might explain his parents to Sarah, but Sarah stood and gave them both an affectionate pat. "You two run along now. I'm sure you have lots to talk about. I'm going to rest."

The two left the main house and when they reached the meadow, they spread their jackets on the ground and sat in the sun. For a while neither one spoke.

"Devon," Jesseree finally said. "I'm sorry."

He looked surprised. "For what?"

"For burning down the cabin. And the last time we were together I was totally unreasonable. I owe you so much and I repaid you with some stupid ego trip."

"But I owe you," he insisted. "You've helped me more than you know. And I apologize. It was wrong of me to tell you what to do. And, Jess, please forget about the fire. Everyone here has." He reached for her hand. "I've got a surprise. But I can't tell you until Thursday."

"A surprise?" Her heart sank. He'd decided to take the post with the brothers! "Tell me now," she pleaded.

"It's too soon. You'll just have to wait." His eyes sparkled in the sun. "If I told you now, then it wouldn't be a surprise."

He teased. But for her this was serious. Leaning over, she tousled his hair. "Come on, Devon. I want to know."

He gently grasped her wrist. Pulling her fingers to his lips he brushed them tenderly. "I've missed you, Jesseree. More than I've ever missed anyone."

She longed to fall into his arms and stay there, wrapped in the tenderness of his embrace. But something held her back. "I've missed you too," she whispered, while her heart sang, *you'll never know how much.*

The next few days were spent getting ready for the big event. Jesseree and Ana worked long hours in the kitchen.

Sarah spent the mornings helping them. Afternoons, she worked with Sebastian and Devon setting up rooms for workshops.

John and the other carpenters temporarily halted their work on the new cabin to build booths in the meadow.

Mary and the dairy boys had gone to Gold Dust down the hill to ask friends of Ahimsa to make room in their homes for the overflow of expected guests.

"Ana," Jesseree wailed. "How will we ever feed them all?"

"Seems impossible, doesn't it?" Ana whisked crumbs from the counter. "Every year I wonder the same thing. But somehow we manage. We always have enough. Students from Gold Dust come up and bring food." She gave the simmering chutney another firm stir. "Jess, before it gets too crowded around here, I want you to know how much I've enjoyed having you as a room-mate. These last few weeks have been great."

Jesseree looked surprised. "Really? I thought I've been crowding you, but being with you has really helped me. Dealing with the fire and all."

"That fire is history," Ana said firmly. "Let's just en-joy today—this minute."

Jesseree wiped her hands on her apron. She went to Ana and gave her a hug. "I want you to know how much I appreciate your friendship. And thanks for listening when I've talked endlessly about Devon."

"I saw you with him in the meadow yesterday," said Ana. "Did you tell him how you feel?"

"I don't think I should." Jess gazed out the window. "Not for a while. I hope he feels the same way about me. At times I think I see it in his eyes." She sighed deeply. "When he touches me, my heart almost explodes."

Ana offered a knowing smile. "I believe you're in love, all right."

Jesseree turned back to chopping apples. "Devon has a surprise for me. He said he'd tell me on Thursday. I believe he's decided to go." She reached for a carrot and split it with a knife. "You'd think I wouldn't want him to leave—it's hard to explain but part of me wants him to work on those scrolls." She looked up. "Strange, huh? I must really love him because I want him to fulfill his dream—not mine."

"That's beautiful," said Ana. "I've known Devon for a long time. From the way he looked at you yesterday, I'd say he's decided to stay."

An uncertainty crossed Jesseree's face. "I'm not sure that would be the right decision. A feeling deep down inside of me says the way to hold Devon is to let him go. I don't know where that feeling comes from, but it's strong."

❧❧❧

On Sunday, enrollment day, the members of Ahimsa held a welcoming tea for the guest speakers. The retreat buzzed with excitement and, by late afternoon, people gathered in the meadow to discuss important issues.

Monday morning classes and workshops began. The downstairs of the big house had room for four workshops. Chairs, benches, and pads arranged around the meadow made room for two more.

By the middle of the week, after attending work-shops presented by visiting professors, teachers, and cler-gymen, Jesseree grappled with the decision whether or not to return to her job at the agency. She'd been serious-ly reading through pamphlets and brochures gathered from each session. So many causes needed personal commitments. She hoped, sometime in the future, to be able to give hers. The problem, which one?

She watched films about world hunger and thought about flying to Africa. She viewed slides of baby seals being slaughtered, and, with tears filling her eyes, she mentally sailed off to Newfoundland with Greenpeace. Finally, she decided until she found her niche, she would stay at Ahimsa and support her brothers and sisters here who were striving to preserve this spaceship called Earth.

After lunch on Wednesday, she pulled Sarah aside and told her how she felt.

Sarah encouraged her. "That's wonderful, dear. Your life will dramatically change once you commit to ser-vice."

"I'll ask Grandma for my inheritance. It's a year ear-ly, but if you help me explain to her—"

"Of course, I will. You won't have a problem with Alice. She only wants what's best for you." Sarah reached into the pocket of her skirt and pulled out an en-velope. "Before I forget this letter came for you. Sebas-tian asked me to deliver it. I peeked at the return address. It's from your friend Maureen."

Jesseree removed a typed page with the agency's heading. She scanned the sheet. "Great," she exclaimed. "Maureen's coming up Friday after work. She read about the conference on a billboard in a health food store and she's made arrangements to attend classes on Saturday."

Thursday afternoon, Devon, accompanied by an older man, approached Jesseree at a booth on the meadow having a discussion with a woman from Greenpeace. "Excuse me," Devon said to the visiting woman. "Jesseree, I would like you to meet someone."

Jesseree glanced up at the tall man, judging him to be a business man in his mid-sixties, dressed expensively, but casually.

When their eyes met, she caught her breath. Before Devon had a chance to introduce them, she knew.

"Jesseree, this is my father, Mathew Pearson."

The older man's face broke into a smile as he held out his hand.

She grasped his hand and smiled uncertainly. "What a lovely surprise."

"I warned you," Devon said. "Now you know why I asked you to wait."

Relief spread through her. A lovely surprise. But what about Sarah? Jesseree searched the crowd. Did Sarah know Mathew was here?

Sarah stood on the porch of the main house talking to a group of students. When Jesseree spotted her laughing and obviously enjoying herself, she glanced back at

Mathew. "We're so happy you could come." She reached for Devon's hand. "You must be thrilled."

Devon nodded. "I called." He looked over at his father and smiled. "Dad had few free days. When I told him the happening here this week, he flew into Reno from Virginia last night. A friend of mine picked him up at the airport and drove him here."

Jesseree looked back at the house but couldn't spot Sarah. "Does Sarah know your father's here?" She avoided Mathew's eyes. Would he connect the name with his long ago love?

"I haven't seen her," Devon glanced around. "But when I do, I'll introduce them."

Sarah suddenly appeared from the crowd. "There you two are," she called. She gasped when she saw Mathew.

"Star," Mathew whispered in disbelief.

Sarah reached for his hands. "Mathew."

A light shone in Mathew's eyes. Without another word to Devon or Jess, they turned and left arm in arm, making their way through the crowd as they cut across the meadow, letting the years fall away behind them.

Devon, stunned, stood motionless until Jesseree took his arm. "Come on." She pulled him along. "Let's go down to the river. I have something to tell you."

She watched Sarah and Mathew disappear up the path toward the plateau. "It looks like this Thursday is full of surprises."

Chapter 24

Devon, confused and feeling light headed, followed Jesseree as she made her way down the dirt path to Bhakti, their private little beach. His father's voice repeatedly echoed through his mind. Star, he'd called Sarah, Star. They knew each other. Why hadn't he been told? "Jesseree," he called after her. "Wait up. I need to know what's going on."

"Hold on," she called back. "We'll be there in a minute."

The hill leveled off and she took off at a run. He tried to keep up but his knees felt weak. His father and Sarah? No! She wouldn't have deceived him all these years.

When Jesseree reached the river bank, she dropped to the sand and slipped off her shoes.

"Let's dip our feet in the cold water. It might clear our heads."

How could she be so cheerful? If he lived a hundred more years he'd never forget the look on his father's face when Sarah came out of that crowd. And Sarah! Breathless as a young girl, calling his father Mathew.

When he reached the sand, Devon plopped down Indian style and frowned. The dark eyes of his mother, tormented and filled with pain, flashed through his mind.

Jesseree angled a look at him. "Devon," she began. "I'm going to tell you a story and I want you to listen with your heart. Sit back and try to relax because it's going to take a while. Just remember that Sarah loves you— and so does your father." She hesitated and studied her hands. "I know you're confused but maybe when I finish…"

She narrated the story of Sarah and Mathew, beginning with their first meeting at the USO, explaining how they fell in love in just three short weeks. She went on listing the reasons Sarah had for not marrying Mathew then she followed Sarah's life through until India, ending with the letter left at the hotel desk.

"When Sarah saw you with your father at the embassy, she knew it would be impossible to meet him alone. Even for a few hours. She could never do that to you and your mother. There was no betrayal. She still loved your dad, but their relationship had ended long before he met your mother."

Devon closed his eyes. "And what about now? Did Sarah ever plan to tell me?"

"I asked her about that before we drove up here. She said she would wait for direction." Jesseree's face flushed. "Maybe I'm way out of bounds, but when they left us back there, somehow I felt it was my place to explain their connection." She placed her hand on his knee. "I know it hurts. Must be an awful shock." She stood and looked down at him. "If this had happened to me, I'd need time alone. I'm leaving now and I'll be at Ana's cabin later if you need me."

Devon stood. "I can only .imagine how difficult this was for you to tell me. I'm angry and hurt." He looked down. "But now after you've explained, maybe…" He hesitated and shook his head, bewildered. "Mathew and Star."

"Oh, Devon." She turned and ran up the path, glancing back only once before continuing on.

Devon sat back down. Why hadn't his mother asked his father to explain? Why hadn't he? He stared at the water tumbling over the smooth rocks. At least he had forgiven his father before he knew Star's identity. He must admire himself for that. But now after hearing their story—he shook his head slowly, realizing there had been nothing to forgive.

The afternoon sun streamed through the pine branches, making uneven golden stripes across the water. Regaining his balance, he ventured out across the slick rocks until he came to the first big boulder. He sat down on the flat surface a few minutes before he slipped into the deep pool below, soaking his cotton clothes. When his feet touched bottom he let out a cry of relief, raised his arms, and jumped into the air. As he splashed down, he lay back in the cold water, floating, washing away old negative feelings, baptizing himself into a new consciousness of joy.

Chapter 25

Sarah sat on her bed and watched Jesseree struggle with the length of green silk, as she attempted to drape it just right for the Indian Feast. Women guests who shared the dorm—dressed in vivid colored dresses and pants, ready for the celebration downstairs—had left over an hour ago.

"I don't know what happened out there on the green today," Sarah apologized. "But when I saw Mathew this morning I forgot everything. I realize now that when we turned and wandered off like that without a word to Devon, it put you in an awkward position." She got up. "Here, let me help you with that." She unwound the fabric from around Jesseree's waist then let it slip from her hands. When she bent over to pick it up, she held the small of her back. "I'm a bit stiff from hiking that hill to Eagle's Point, but it was worth it. However, leaving you to clear things up with Devon, well that was inexcusable."

Jesseree waved it off. "It worked out all right. Don't you always say that events are in cosmic order?"

"True. But in my self-centeredness, I shirked my responsibility." Sarah looked thoughtful. "I'll make it up to you, Jess."

"Don't worry about me. Devon's hurt and confused. That's the hard part. But when I left him at the beach, I felt he'd already started working through the confusion. I'm really not too concerned about him. When you and Mathew had lunch with him today how did it go?"

"Awkward at first. He was a bit distant. But after we explained the past, he began to warm up. Mathew had difficulty believing that Devon and I had known each other all of these years. His regret is that we didn't all meet sooner."

"That's for sure. Is he still single?"

"Yes. He never remarried. His business has been his life."

"Now he can add you and Devon to the rest of his life."

Jesseree crossed to the window. "Look at that full moon. The second one this month. A Blue Moon. It's been said to fill the darkness with mystery and romance." She gazed out into the night a long moment before she turned around. "Did Devon happen to mention the Hima-layas to his dad?"

"Not while I was there."

"Does Mathew know?"

"If he does, he didn't say anything to me, and they didn't discuss it over lunch." Sarah was obviously in pain with her back. Jesseree went to her and worked the heel of her hand into the tight muscle. "That's it," Sarah said. "Right there." She groaned a little as Jesseree massaged. "When this celebration's over, Mathew's going back to Sausalito with me to spend a few days. He says now that we've found each other again, he'll never lose track of me. He's already making plans for us to be together over the Holidays."

"Then we better get this kink out." Jesseree kneaded her knuckles harder. "Mathew will probably want you to join him later for a stroll under that Blue Moon."

When Jesseree finished, Sarah sighed and wiggled her shoulders. "You have that magic touch. I've been wondering. Did your friend arrive?"

"Maureen? Yes. She's been helping Klaus Hoffman all day. You know, the German physicist. She says she feels comfortable with a man like him. His strict disci-pline gives her a sense of security." Jesseree laughed. "She says that now, but just let him show some authority and she'll drop him like a hot dumpling."

Sarah smoothed the raw green silk out on the bed be-fore picking it up in both hands. "Now." She stood in front of Jesseree. "No more chatter. You must get dressed." She wound the material around Jesseree. "The trick is to bring this end over to the center." She patted Jesseree's midriff. "Press your arm right here. That will hold everything in place." She reached for a green belt then slipped it around Jesseree's waist. When she finished draping, she pushed the other end of the fabric over Jesseree's shoulder being careful not to let it fall below her hipline. "You can leave the end to fall loose. Or you can bring it up and cover your head." She stepped back. "What will it be?"

Jesseree slipped on the filigree earrings. "It looks fine the way it is." She lifted a length of gold chiffon from the bed. "I'll use this for a veil." She placed it over her smooth chignon. "How does it look?"

"Beautiful," Sarah said. "Wait until Devon sees you. I've decided not to wear my sari tonight. I thought it might make Mathew a bit uncomfortable."

"What about Devon?"

"With you two, it's different. Devon will be thrilled. It's rare to see a blonde beauty wearing an authentic Indian sari."

Music floated up from downstairs. Jesseree crossed over to the door. "Sounds like a harp."

"It's Mary," Sarah said. "She plays like an angel."

Jesseree stepped down on the stairs. "I'm going to peek."

"Just go." Sarah motioned her on. "I still have to

change into my long skirt. Don't wait for me. I'll find you later."

Jesseree nodded as she lifted the gold-bordered hem of the sari. Her sandaled feet moved noiselessly down the stairs. Below, the room was packed with students and guests. Wearing a sheer pink gown, Mary strummed the harp. Her long golden hair fell in a cloud across her shoulders, as her strong fingers plucked the strings.

In the center of the room John and Paul were having a discussion with the German, Klaus Hoffman. At a long oak table under the window, Maureen helped Ana fill dishes with Eastern delicacies made weeks before.

The harp music suddenly became a wondrous wind that lifted Jesseree's mood and moved her majestically down the open staircase. She felt like a queen—a priestess. For one glorious moment she was Isis—Cleopatra—Delilah, bound to her temptress sisters by the gold and green cloth.

Her eyes searched the room for Devon and found him standing alone near the doorway. A warmth rose from her breast, surging up to her cheeks. He stood absolutely still and met her gaze openly, revealingly. Before her foot touched the bottom step, he moved toward her, weaving his way through the crowd, his saffron tunic flashing. They met and he took her hand in his and, with gentle insistence, led her across the room and out through the open door.

On the porch, small groups of students and teachers

spoke quietly, but Devon made no move to join them. With a firm hold on Jesseree's arm, he escorted her down the steps and onto the path that led to the meadow. She felt a strong vibration from him as they walked along together. Stars above blinked erratically, adding magic to the moonlit night.

Devon stopped abruptly and faced her. "You're probably wondering why I brought you here." His voice trembled. "I need to speak to you alone."

She didn't wonder, she knew. He was going to tell her that he must leave. He had solved the problem with his father and now felt free to join the brothers in good conscience.

His eyes searched her face then focused on her lips "You're so lovely." He leaned over and brushed her mouth with his. Her eyes widened at his intimate touch and she backed away.

"Jesseree. What is it? I thought you felt—"

He drew her back and she let him. He covered her mouth again with a kiss that stirred her soul. Reaching up, she slipped her arms around his neck, returning his kiss with all the passion she'd been suppressing. How long they were entwined, their souls blending, wrapped in their blanket of splendor, she didn't know. But when she pushed away again she said, "Devon. Wait. Is this what you really want?"

"More than anything," he murmured.

"But you're leaving."

"But I'm not," he said. "Let someone else go to India. I want to stay here with you. I love you."

As the full Blue Moon climbed the cloudless sky lighting their space with a mystical glow, Jesseree breathed deeply in an attempt to cool her fevered mind. More than anything, she longed to throw her arms around him. Tell him that's what she wanted too. Tell him to whisk her off to his cabin to make endless love. But when she looked into his eyes, she was jarred back to reality. She knew that his work with the brothers took precedence over everything. No matter how desperately they wanted each other now, their love would have to wait.

One word from her and he would stay. One wrong word and the work on the scrolls in the Himalayas would have to wait. Devon's dream would be unfulfilled. If he didn't go now, he would regret his decision later. And if he didn't, she would. She knew this instinctively—intuitively—and karmically.

She took another deep breath of the night air. But the cooling breath she sought for relief unmercifully turned to molten lava as it flowed through her veins. Never before had she known such fire. Unlike the steady flame of the candle she religiously lit at twilight, this flame raged against her intellect like a blazing torch, threatening to destroy her will. She fought to center herself, to bring some semblance of calmness to her confused mind.

Devon lifted her veil and slipped the pins from her hair. Thick strands of silver fell to her shoulders and he filled his hands with the shimmering mass. "I adore you, Jesseree," he said. "You're my jewel of desire."

Jewel of desire. His words struck a distant chord. She let go of all reason and surrendered to the rapture of the moment, responding passionately to his kisses, until a strong breeze brushed her face and she regained her sanity. "I can't. No. There will be time enough when you return. You must go." She spoke the releasing words quickly before she lost her courage. She gripped his arms in an attempt to make him understand. "No matter how long it takes, Devon, I'll be waiting. Even if it takes forever."

A harsh step on the gravel path caused them both to turn. A lone figure approached and stepped from the shadows. An ominous cloud engulfed Jesseree as she strained to make out who it was.

Jacob! Dear God!

She let go of Devon's arms as her heart rushed to her throat.

For a moment Jacob stood motionless in a shaft of moonlight. A glint of metal in his clenched fist turned her heart to ice. "Found you," he said, slurring his words. Steadying the gun with both hands, he squinted. "You can't leave me, Jess. No way."

Behind her, Jesseree could feel Devon's body, tense and strong.

"Come on," Jacob ordered, shaking the gun. "Stand over here."

The tone of his voice filled her with terror. In one

quick move, Devon leaped in front of her, shielding her from Jacob and his weapon.

Jacob's eyes glowed with loathing. "You son-of—"

Devon moved cautiously forward. "Give me the gun. Don't be a fool."

"Who're you calling a fool? You—you—" Jacob stammered. Then he screamed out, "Jesus freak!" He lunged at Devon, reaching around him for Jesseree. Devon's arms flew up blocking him. To Jesseree's horror a shot rang out shattering the night and her mind into a million pieces.

For what seemed an eternity, the two men stood clutching each other. Then Devon slumped to the earth.

Chapter 26

In that terrible moment the world stopped for Jesseree. The stage lights of life dimmed as the moon disappeared behind a dark cloud. Jesseree stared at Jacob with disbelief and horror as he let the gun drop from his hand.

He stared at her blankly. "I didn't plan this." His voice broke through the armor of silence that enclosed her. Screaming, she dropped to her knees beside Devon pulling him to her breast.

Within minutes, they were surrounded by people. Jesseree could feel Sarah on the ground beside her gently pulling on her arm. "Let him go, dear—let us have him." Sarah's voice broke. "Please, Jesseree. We can't help him if you won't let him go."

Jesseree looked down at Devon's face. His eyes were closed. Blood poured through his thin shirt from the wound in his chest. She'd tried to let him go—give him up. She looked up at the blurred faces around her and shook her head. She pulled Devon even closer, rocking him in her arms while the world reeled about her. Go away, she silently screamed. He's mine! She pressed her face against his pale brow as Sebastian and Mathew knelt down in front of her.

"Jess, please," Sebastian pleaded. "Let us take him."

Mathew put his arms around her and tried to lift her.

"No—no," she cried, her voice echoing through the trees. "Don't take him from me."

With gentle force, they pried her arms from his back and carefully lifted him. Jesseree grabbed for the hem of his tunic, but Anasuya and Sarah held her back. She struggled against them, sobbing and begging them both to let her go, but they held her firmly as the men rushed Devon up the path to the house. Sarah whispered something to Ana, before she quickly followed after the men. When Sarah had gone, Maureen stepped from the crowd and took Sarah's space next to her friend.

"Oh, Jess," She wrapped her jacket and her arms around her. "What can I do?"

Anasuya, with tears streaming from her eyes, said, "Let's get her back to my cabin. Come on, Jess, let's go." The two women supported her, one on each side as they half-carried her across the meadow.

Jesseree, sobbing, turned and looked back. The moon passed from behind the black cloud and its luminous light flooded the ground where Devon had lain. The crowd had spread out now except for a group of men holding Jacob's arms securely behind him. She watched as they pushed him into the back seat of a car, slammed the doors, and sped away.

Chapter 27

Jesseree struggled up the mountain's winding path to the plateau, clutching Ana's jacket to her chest. From below, Maureen hollered for her to come back. Dried weeds and bushes snagged and ripped at the green sari as Jesseree continued on, climbing higher, ignoring Maureen's call. When she reached the plateau, she crawled over to the big oak and lay there gasping.

"Jess—Jess, please come back," Maureen's voice wailed. "Jess—e—ree. I can't find you in the dark."

Jesseree clapped her hands over her ears and lay there, panting like a frightened animal, whimpering and talking to herself, bargaining with whatever powers that be to save Devon.

She pulled herself up to her knees, dug her fingernails into the rough bark, and hugged the trunk of the old tree.

"It's my entire fault," she cried to the bare limbs above. "I've caused this. Don't make Devon pay."

"Jess—e—ree," the call came again. "Let me help. Tell me where you are."

Jesseree stopped crying for a moment as anger flashed across her grieving mind. How dare they stop her from being with him? These people had no idea how much Devon meant to her. They were insane if they expected her to stay in Ana's cabin. He needed her now. And she needed to be by his side. If anything happened to him—

She began to weep. At first softly, childlike, then her entire body shook with deep sobs. By now Maureen's calls for her had stopped. The night grew still. She leaned over and looked down the side of the mountain to the lighted house. Maybe they were right to take Devon away. After what Jacob had done, she didn't deserve to be with him.

Moments later feeling desperate, she scrambled to her feet, attempted to pull herself together and make her way back down there. She'd find a way to get to him and, if they tried to stop her, she'd storm the door, demand to see him. Her shoulders sagged as a tremendous weariness washed over her, and she slumped to the ground, defeated. Bunching up her coat, she laid her head down. She would stay up here and keep a watch. Night sounds began to lull her, and soon her eyelids fluttered and closed. A fitful sleep overtook her and she snuggled into a groove at the base of the tree. The night settled in around her.

A man in a robe appeared at her feet. He knelt on one knee and pressed a finger between her brows on the center of her forehead. Jesseree immediately opened her eyes. When she saw the hem of the white robe she pushed herself up. The monk. He placed a silver goblet in her hand.

"Help me," she cried, clutching at his robe. "Something terrible has happened."

"I know, my daughter," he said in a steady voice. "Drink of this. It will help." He supported her shoulders as he lifted the goblet to her trembling lips.

Jesseree took a sip then pushed his hand away. "They've got Devon down there," she sobbed, motioning to the house. "Jacob shot him and I think—I think…" Her voice faded. "I think he's dying." She slumped to the ground and buried her face in her jacket. When she looked up, the monk still extended the goblet.

"Daughter, drink this elixir." He helped her to sit up. This time she accepted the goblet and drank.

In an instant, she found herself standing by his side, gazing into his eyes. He pointed toward the ground. She turned to see her body lying there in a deep sleep. "We will leave your pain and your gross form behind for now. It is time for your pilgrimage to the Temple of the Sun. Come."

Feeling strangely refreshed, and detached, she stared at her body sleeping in the groove beneath the tree. The monk held out his hand and she grasped it, eager now to join him. His light form moved effortlessly up the rocky incline and she followed along, infused with newfound energy.

When they reached Eagle's Point, the monk stopped and stood on a flat surface covered with heavy brush. Behind the growth was a cave. Bending low, they entered a small opening. On the other side of the entrance, they straightened and walked on until they reached an arched door at the far end of the cave.

The monk slipped two fingers through a brass loop and the door slowly opened. Filtered light shone down on a garden filled with fragrant lavender flowers growing near the base of a bubbling stone fountain. They passed the garden and the fountain until they reached a cobblestone path. A waterfall next to the path cascaded over white rocks and green moss, emptying into a bottomless pool filled with pink lotus flowers.

He motioned to the flat polished rocks spaced like stairs on each side of the falls. "This is the way."

Jesseree looked up. The steps appeared to be endless. Higher and higher until they disappeared into a white mist.

Across from where she stood, on the far side of the falls, a procession of monks, their heads covered with hoods, descended through the mist.

"Ommm—Ommm." The vibration of their chant shook the ground.

When Jesseree's monk on their side of the waterfalls motioned for her to follow, she did so eagerly, as he climbed the steps and guided her upward. At one point he turned. "Are you willing to continue?"

"Yes," she whispered. "I am willing to follow wherever you lead me."

They climbed onward and upward. He stopped and waited for her to reach him then led her over a small arched bridge that spanned the falls, to a heavy wooden door, open and waiting. Inside, Jesseree found herself at the entrance to a huge hall with a giant transparent dome that opened to the starry night.

At the far end of the hall, surrounded by a luminous glow, stood a long carved table with seven chairs. On a platform behind the table, rose a gold alter. Above the alter, an enormous dark mirror held her gaze. The monk stepped to the center of the room and pointed to two purple cushioned chairs. He sat and motioned for her to sit by his side. Above, in the opening of the dome, a full moon drifted in, settled, and floated in a sea of black sky. A sudden shaft of light poured down. As it grew in intensity, it illuminated the mirror screen.

"Your story will unfold here. You will now be allowed to glimpse past lives."

She stared up at the screen, fascinated as galaxies and universes swirled in a myriad of colors. The room dissolved around them as they were lifted out through the screen into another realm, propelled through space, voyagers bound on a cosmic excursion.

"Our first stop will be the Great Central Sun." The monk pointed ahead. "It lies beyond the sun of your planet where creation began eons ago, outside the confines of time and space. Where you and Devon, representing the feminine and masculine of One Soul stood before Alpha and Omega. You vowed to bring golden energy from the spirit plane to planet Earth. Thus you were divided, one flame into two—Twin Flames. Divided not separated. You left this stratus with identical spiritual blueprints, endowed with great power which would enable you to accomplish this tremendous task."

They circled the brilliant sun. Solar flames leaped high. "Touch them," the monk directed, gathering the flames to his center. "This is your Divine Inheritance. These flames will strengthen you for the tasks that await you."

Jesseree reached out and pulled them to her, absorbing all the energy she could hold.

When the cycle around the sun was completed, they flew off in a cloud of glory, racing on to a far off planet. As they grew closer, she could see a tremendous upheaval. A section of the planet in chaos as water flooded the land.

"This is Earth," the monk said. "Ahead is the continent where an ancient civilization lived in perfection while it looked to The Source for light and direction. But soon men and women created conditions so destructive they brought havoc on themselves. When they lost their land, they wailed in misery as they also lost their physical bodies. That wailing has prevailed throughout the ages."

Jesseree and the monk hovered above as huge waves rose and swallowed masses of land. They watched as screaming inhabitants disappeared into the sea. Old fears clutched Jesseree's heart as she stared down at the cataclysm.

"It was here, daughter, that you first took your gross form. You were spawned by the Rain God Tectal and a high priestess of the Teaching Temple. Your mother then, is the woman you know now as Sarah.

"Devon, a scribe was generated by the love of two highly spiritual beings who struggled to raise him by the laws of Light. You met at the temple. He went there daily to record the Laws of Peace dictated by the Council. His destiny then was to chronicle Divine Truth to the scrolls but leave before the continent destroyed itself. You both ignored his ordained duty to accompany those scrolls to the safety of the East where at an appointed time he would be led to reveal their Truth to the world.

"As the appointed time neared for him to leave the submerging continent, you let fear overcome you, daughter. You were given power. You misused it. As a child of an Earth mother and a God father, you were expected to carry on the work of the temple. You were sent to lead backward tribes into the Truth. Your destiny, to teach them trades to build an empire. A New Age Empire of Peace.

"Your half-brother, now known to you as Jacob, also son of the high-priestess, was to rule by your side. Through this alliance he would learn the meaning of compassion. You were to teach him with patience and unconditional love. Your obsession with Devon, your Twin Flame, prevented you from carrying this through. It led you away from the guiding voice that whispered deep in your heart. You used your power to distract Devon, bringing disaster to all three of you.

"On the Akashic record of the Celestial Hierarchy, you three are written as the Karmic Triad. Throughout coming incarnations, you three have been given the chance to work out your karmic debt."

"Is it too late?" Jesseree murmured.

"Never. Your soul does not keep time. It merely records growth. Had you remained in harmony, you would have realized that you and your twin flame could never be separated. You are cosmic lovers. Because of fear, you both experienced a sense of separation. Because of this you have lived incarnation after incarnation, unable to complete the work for which you were sent."

Jesseree hung her head with remorse.

The cosmic tides turned abruptly, skimming them over the raging waters to the higher plains where massive pyramids were being constructed.

"This is the Land of the Mayas," said the monk. "It was here the three of you fled after your continent was destroyed. You attempted to carry out your destiny to help these tribes attain their highest growth, but you were blocked by negative energy. Your web of deceit held you back. Devon remained a captive of your desire.

"Jacob, angered by your rejection, plotted revenge. He sent Devon on an expedition to the south to a country you now call Guatemala. Certain that Devon would be killed by rival tribes or lost in the merciless jungles, he celebrated his victory prematurely. Drunk with power, he visited your chambers demanding the love he had been denied. When you refused, he disclosed his devious scheme. Devon did return. And with him were packets of precious stones found in a quarry deep within the jungles. He came to you and placed the jewels in your hands.

"Jacob, seething with envy and greed, ordered members of the expedition tortured in hopes of gaining direction to the quarry, but the guides were your loyal servants. One night in a state of rage, he ordered the guards to pull Devon from his bed. They bound his hands and feet and threw him in Cenote, the sacrificial well."

"No—no," Jesseree cried out. "I can't bear it. I've been such a fool."

"The loss of him left you bereft and ill," the monk continued. "You stayed in your quarters for months. When you finally emerged and faced the people, you were heavy with Devon's child.

"Jacob left the temple to search for the lost quarry and never returned. You lived on alone to rule the Yucatan for forty more years, helping the tribes with the aid of your son, Quetzlcoatl, the most powerful figure to live on that continent. You were unable to complete your mission to its fullest, but your son became a great civilizer and lawgiver—a man filled with understanding for his fellow men and women.

"When your followers finally laid your physical body to rest in a tomb beneath the temple, during the funeral one of the treasured stones, given to you by Devon years before, was placed in your mouth. From that time until the present you have been known as Chalchihuite, precious beloved priestess, named for the carved green stones you call jade."

Strong feelings from the past stirred Jesseree's soul. Faces of those who had loved her in that primitive time appeared one by one in the clouds above her. They gazed down with adoration, filling her heart with regret.

"Come," said the monk. "There is no time for sadness. We have much to see." With another quick turn, they flew back over an ocean to a colony in the desert. Jesseree recognized the palace from her dream with the open ceiling and large columns.

"This is Egyo, now known as Egypt." Pyramids rose up below them. "In this incarnation you lived in this palace. You were part of a large royal family. At this time, Jacob was your cousin, a quarrelsome, lazy youth. When your father, the king, died, Jacob ruled and chose to have you rule by his side. You gave your heart to a staff member of The Great Temple of Knowledge. An evolved soul preparing for his initiation ceremony. Once again you seduced him, making it impossible for him to achieve his goal. When Jacob was informed of your action, another killing took place. Once more as in the past, Devon's blood stained Jacob's hands."

A melody drifted up from the palace. The bearded face from her dream appeared. A sharp stab of pain pierced Jesseree's heart and she experienced her loss once again as her beloved tried to lift her through the Celestial Gates.

"You chose once more to follow your passion, daughter. Another lifetime spent in sorrow."

Jesseree's head bent low. "Yes. It is all clear."

"We go now to your last incarnation," the monk continued. "A time of rough, rugged men filled with the fever for gold." They flew across the ocean over valleys and mountains until they reached the familiar terrain of the Foothills and the Yuba River. "Gold was placed upon the Earth to purify, vitalize, and balance the atomic structure of the world. Not for greed." He pointed below. "Not for ornamentation and exchange."

Jesseree recognized the town of Downieville and trembled, recalling the horror she'd experienced there. The same scene spread out beneath her now. The hanging and the funeral. Instantly, she knew, even before the monk explained, who hung from the scaffold. Who lay in the pine coffin.

"Yes, daughter. Another tragedy for you as you watched Jacob hang for his murderous deed. However, this time you understood that the killing could have been prevented. Prevented, if you had only let go."

She nodded slowly, remembering.

"Devon tried again to reach the lost scrolls. He was given the chance to take passage on a ship to China by a monk who lived on the property you now call Ahimsa. A fine student and devoted follower of the Holy Man from the East, Devon almost completed his destiny until your desire held him back."

Jesseree flinched as the trap door was sprung on the scaffold. The young girl fainted. Devon's mother, Sarah, poured out her grief as she followed behind her dead son's casket.

"Jacob, young and greedy for gold, found a large vein in the river. Confident that his riches would win you, he proposed marriage. When you told him of your love for Devon, he became enraged. You quarreled and Devon intervened. Jacob stabbed him, blotting out both of their lives as well as yours. For you never regained your physical strength. You remained an invalid. A bitter old woman, bedridden until death."

Darkness engulfed them. When it lifted, they were back in the long hall looking up at the screen. The moon continued its climb, on past the dome, leaving the mirror screen dark once more. A blue light dimly lit the room and the room became still.

Jesseree now understood the true meaning of her life. The truth about love. For the first time since the recent awful scene back on the meadow, she wondered about Jacob.

"Once more he has been caught up in the negative," the monk said, as if he read her thoughts. "He was given the chance in this lifetime to right his wrongs. Summoned before this Council in his dreams, he was shown what was required of him. He did not choose to heed our words. However on this eve, he did not premeditate murder. The weapon he carried he used to manipulate, not to kill. Murder was not in his heart. But like a needle drawn to a magnet, he played out the old scene again. The triad of you, Devon, and Jacob.

"Although on the Cosmic Ladder his evolvement rests on a step below you and Devon, he still makes progress. In this incarnation, he has gone past his dark desires for material gain. However, his self-serving demands must still be dealt with. We do not ask you to condone Jacob's deed on this night, daughter, but we do ask that you forgive him."

Jesseree bowed her head. All the scenes from ancient times crowded her mind, crushing her heart with regret.

"Do not suffer over what has passed," said the monk. "The seemingly sorrowful events of your endless life were only stations for growth. It is at the lowest ebb of life when the seed of selflessness buried deep within a heart sprouts forth."

He placed his hand over hers and she felt his strength. It filtered through her like gold dust settling into the valleys of her grief.

"But what about Devon now. Will he live?"

"He will live on Earth to fulfill his destiny in this incarnation. He will transcribe the scrolls, and in so doing, proclaim to the world the great secrets of peace, learned but not practiced in Atlantis. If this civilization chooses to listen, then he will launch a new and glorious golden age."

Jesseree sighed, relieved.

"You, daughter, have a destiny to fulfill also." The monk looked deeply into her eyes. "You will return to the land of the Mayas and search for the quarries filled with precious stones. The jade stone for which you have been named. When you locate these earthly treasures, you will deliver maps of these ancient sites to heads of government presiding over those middle countries. They will use your gifts to feed and clothe their people and you will help them. At a time ordained, when Devon returns from the holy mountains in the east, you will return here also. You will be together again."

Together again. Jesseree's heart sang. She turned to the monk. "But when? Where do I go?"

"No need for concern, daughter. Whenever you create silence, you will be guided. Whenever you are in the midst of turmoil, be still and know.

A silver haze formed at the end of the hall. "The Council is assembling. Prepare, daughter, to stand before them."

Jesseree straightened her shoulders. "I am ready."

Seven radiant beings in long blue robes appeared on the platform below the mirror. They circled the golden altar then wound their way down the steps to the carved table. As if in rhythm to a cosmic pulse, they took their places one by one.

The monk touched Jesseree on the arm and they both stood. After a long silence, the walls reverberated from a clang of an unseen cymbal. The Council member seated in the center lifted his hand and held up a thick tapered crystal. He placed it on the table before him next to an open book and the room lit up.

"You have been brought, daughter, by your guide to be shown the glories of the higher life." His voice rang out. "These truths are shown only to those beings who can view them and return to Earth to resume their life. You have proven to the Council you are ready. In your present incarnation, you have learned that whoever seeks to exist anywhere in creation without selfless love cannot survive. By turning within, you have succeeded in conquering the destructive passions of former lives. You have come to realize the true meaning of love. Your unselfishness toward your Twin Flame has paid your karmic debt." He slammed the huge book shut. "The pages of the past are closed."

A chorus of voices rose. "So be it—so be it."

"You have allowed Divine Love to flow through you," he continued. "You and your Twin Flame are united for eternity."

The Council turned when drapes behind the altar opened revealing massive bronze doors. The doors swung open and Devon stood there edged in light. He wore a *sarcedotal* robe and his feet were wrapped with strips of gold. An amulet of the All Seeing Eye hung around his neck from a copper chain.

As he stood there, his aura grew in intensity, charging the air, lifting Jesseree's soul into a realm of spiritual ecstasy. He approached her and she trembled, seeing her own inner face reflected in his eyes. When he reached her side, he placed a matching amulet around her neck and enfolded her into his blazing aura.

She glanced down and her tattered sari had been transformed into shimmering folds of gossamer, dotted with weightless stones of diamonds, sapphires, and rubies. She became a goddess, rising from the sea, bathed in the glory of his eyes.

He looked like a god standing before her, shining golden in celestial splendor. They lingered there until the room faded around them and they rose into space on powerful wings.

Suspended, locked in their cosmic love, they passed through time—time before time—and time beyond time. They merged, filling their souls with light.

Time stopped as a new galaxy burst into being. At last, Jesseree was fulfilled.

Chapter 28

It had been a long night of healing prayers and solemn meditation in the main house, but at last Devon, weak and pale, regained consciousness and whispered, "Jesseree." As he lay on Sarah's bed surrounded by his friends and family, Anasuya came into the room and touched Sarah's shoulder, motioning her aside.

"Maureen can't find Jess. She's been calling for her every hour but Jess doesn't answer."

Through the long night, Sarah's attention had been focused on Devon. Mary, Sebastian, and Mathew were able to stop Devon's bleeding. After they assessed his wound, they made the decision to wait until dawn, rather than attempting to move him down the rutted road to a hospital in the dark.

But now there was Jesseree to think about. This was the second time Ana had come in, her eyes filled with concern to report that Jesseree could not to be found. Sarah got up from the chair. "Does she have her coat with her?"

"That's the first question I asked," said Ana. "Maureen says she grabbed it before she left the cabin."

"Then you stay here and take my place." Sarah motioned to the healing group gathered around Devon's bed. "I'll go outside and help Maureen." She quickly pulled on her heavy sweater. "I believe I know where she went." Sarah left the house as the first silver rays of dawn poured over the mountain top and stepped out onto the porch glistening with frost. Taking a deep breath of the cold air, she made her way down the steps. She huddled into her sweater and pulled the knitted collar up around her neck. Over in the parking area, she could see John and Kapula preparing the van with blankets and pillows making ready to transport Devon to the hospital.

Maureen came running, her hair wild and uncombed. "Sarah, thank God." She nearly fell into Sarah's arms. "I'm so worried."

"She won't freeze," Sarah kept her voice calm. "She has her down jacket."

Maureen stepped back. "But where did she go? Why won't she answer when I call?"

"She's probably too upset. Perhaps she went to sleep. Don't worry. We'll find her." Sarah looked up at the mountain. "It will be light soon enough to find our way up to the plateau. I think she's there."

The two women hurried across to the foot of the path. Sarah stopped, gasped, and looked up. Jesseree was winding her way down the dirt path, flanked by eight white-robed monks carrying candle torches in their raised hands. Her head and shoulders were draped with a white diaphanous cape trimmed in gold braid. An "Ommm" sound from the procession filled the morning air.

"Dear God," Sarah whispered.

"It's Jess," Maureen cried and started up the hill.

Sarah grabbed her arm.

Maureen tried to pull away. "Sarah. Let me go. It's Jess."

Sarah's grip tightened. "Don't you see them?"

"Who?" Maureen said impatiently. "I see Jess."

"The monks in white robes."

Maureen squinted. "Monks?" She looked puzzled. "I just see Jess—and she's okay." She pulled away and started up the hill.

"No." Sarah commanded, raising her hand. "Wait. Let them guide her."

Maureen hesitated then frowned.

As the procession moved slowly down, Sarah's eyes widened. When they reached the end of the path, the monks lifted the sheer cloak from Jesseree's shoulders and held the flaming candles high above her head in trib-ute. Without turning to look back at the holy escort,

Jesseree immediately went to Sarah and Maureen. They both pulled her close.

"Oh, Jess." Maureen slipped off her coat and wrapped it around her shoulders. "Where have you been? It's a wonder you didn't freeze."

Sarah put a finger to her lips, signaling for Maureen to be silent. She watched as the monks ascended the mountain, lighting their way with the torches. When they were out of sight, she turned back to the others. "Come on," she said to Jesseree. "Someone wants to see you."

Together, the three women quickly crossed the meadow. As they stepped up on the porch, Jesseree stopped before going in. "He will be fine," she said, her voice clear and filled with confidence. "Devon will live a long life."

Epilogue

The New Millennium, Asilomar, California:

G lobal communities from all around the nation gathered in the lobby of the conference center waiting in anticipation for the evening symposium soon to be held on the main stage. Old friends, new faces, spiritually integrated thinkers, and activists had attended the all-day sessions led by conference speakers; ministers, authors, artists, professors of world religions, doctors of mind research, conscious living, and Dharma Harata from Delhi, a noted doctor of science, technology, and ecology.

At seven-thirty sharp, the double doors opened to the grand hall. New thinkers—women and men from all walks of life, hands filled with folders and brochures from all-day morning and afternoon sessions, headed for seats to hear Devon Mathews, the dynamic featured speaker of GPM, the Global Peace Movement.

Devon, the man who had spent five years during the early eighties helping the Himalayan brothers to sort through archives, transcribing symbols of ancient scrolls found in an abandoned monastery, now possessed knowledge of the ten vital steps necessary for world peace found in those scrolls.

Earlier, Jesseree Lipton's morning workshop, *ELIM-INATING THE CONCEPT OF FIRST AND THIRD WORLDS*, focused on her international aid organization and the Yucatan geological find of the last century, the principal dig she had led in the early eighties assisted by Maureen and a dedicated group from Green Peace. A phenomenal dig that had won them a Nobel Prize for having done the most thorough work to form a fraternity between nations.

During the early session, she had revealed how they were spiritually directed to dig in an enormous pit where they unearthed precious stones buried eons ago by a previous civilization. And how those same ancient treasures, recently handed over to charitable leaders, were saving the lives of thousands of villagers and would continue to do so throughout the next two decades, providing much needed support of food and clothing to the undernourished children.

A silence fell over the conference hall when Devon, dressed in khaki pants and open collared blue sports shirt strode across the stage. He nodded to the audience, smiled at Jesseree and their teen-age daughter, Sierra, seated in the front row next to their long-time friend Maureen. During the applause, he held out his hand and Jesseree joined him on stage. When she reached his side, she straightened the sleeves of her white cotton embroidered blouse and arranged her notes on the podium. She smiled to herself confidently, silently dedicating this moment to the memory of her mentor Sarah, passed from this plane two years before.

The next hour flew by in the packed hall. Standing stately behind the back row, a very tall man with light curly hair and an extremely high forehead, observed Jesseree and Devon as they took turns recounting their collective meaningful finds over the last twenty years. As they neared the end of their lecture, they both stressed Ahimsa—Jesseree defining in detail the meaning of the Sanskrit word, non-violence, Devon disclosing each strategic steps from the ancient lost scrolls, advising that each seeker already knew the steps in the core of his or her being, but must now refresh, study, and put into physical works, those same transcriptions from millenniums past, in order to preserve our planet Earth.

THE END

About the Author

Norma Lehr, a former nurse and health food store owner from the Bay Area, has four children and five grandchildren and now lives in Auburn, California, in the beautiful Sierra foothills.

She is a multi-genre author of short stories, a middle-grade ghost series, and an adult supernatural novel, *Dark Maiden* (Juno Books, imprint of Wildside Press.)

Her current Abby Reynolds theater mystery series, *Timestep to Murder*, and *Deadly Shuffle* are available from Camel Press and Amazon.